ADVENTURE ISLAND

THE MYSTERY
OF THE WHISTLING CAVES

D0037410

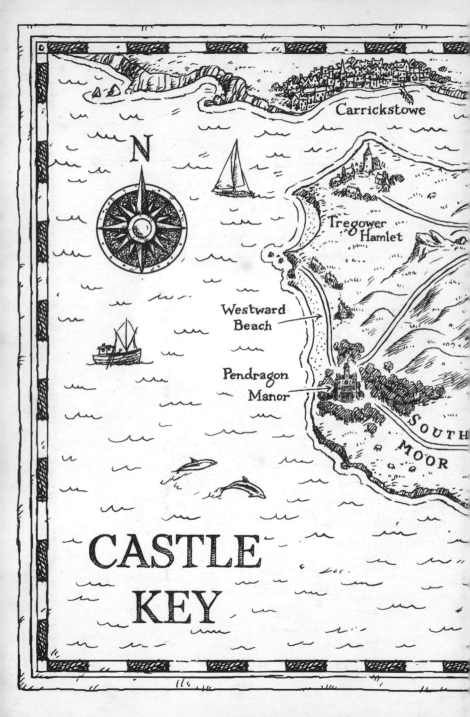

Carrickstowe

N

Tregower
Hamlet

Westward
Beach

Pendragon
Manor

SOUTH
MOOR

CASTLE
KEY

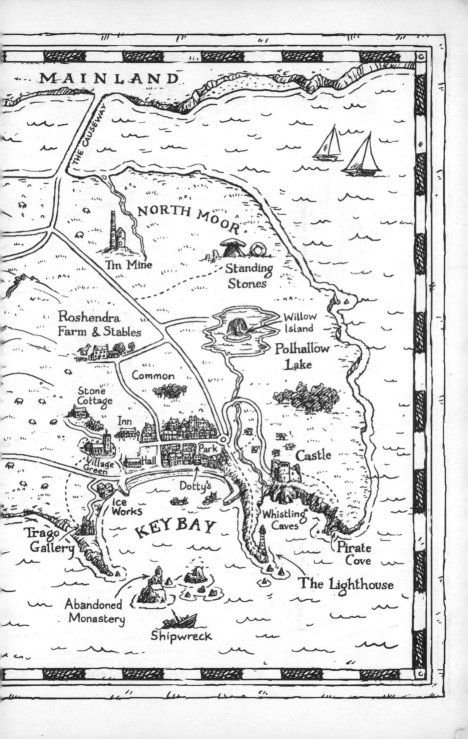

Collect all the Adventure Island *books*

ADVENTURE ISLAND

THE MYSTERY OF THE WHISTLING CAVES

Helen Moss

Illustrated by Leo Hartas

Orion
Children's Books

First published in Great Britain in 2011
by Orion Children's Books
a division of the Orion Publishing Group Ltd
Orion House
5 Upper St Martin's Lane
London WC2H 9EA
An Hachette UK company

5 7 9 10 8 6 4

The Orion Publishing Group's policy is to use papers
that are natural, renewable and recyclable products and made
from wood grown in sustainable forests. The logging and
manufacturing processes are expected to conform to
the environmental regulations of the country of origin.

A catalogue record for this book is
available from the British Library.

ISBN 978 1 4440 0328 4

Printed in Great Britain by Clays Ltd, St Ives plc

For Mac

One

Welcome to Castle Key

Stone Cottage was quite possibly the most boring place Jack Carter had ever seen. The walls were grey, the roof was grey, grey rain was falling from a grey sky; even the pigeons huddling on the chimney were grey and sort of *fed-up* looking.

'You'll have the time of your lives in Castle Key,' Dad said in the car on the way from London to Cornwall. 'Your Uncle Tim and I used to spend summers with

Aunt Kate when we were your age. There're beaches and rock pools and moors and woods. And there's a smashing café on the seafront that does the best fish and chips . . .'

'Smashing'! What kind of word was that? Jack rolled his eyes at his older brother as they drove across the narrow causeway from the mainland to the small island of Castle Key. Scott rolled his back. At least Jack guessed he did. It was hard to actually see Scott's eyes these days; since turning thirteen, he'd been growing his hair long and it flopped over his face like a shabby brown curtain. Dad had been doing the hard sell on this whole super-summer-by-the-seaside experience ever since they left London. But why couldn't he and Scott go with Dad to the rainforests of Central Africa? That's what Jack wanted to know! They'd stay out of the way while Dad was working on his archaeological dig, excavating an ancient settlement. OK, so it was a bit close to a war zone, and there were a few minor problems with malaria and venomous snakes, but, hey, at least they wouldn't drop dead from terminal boredom there.

Aunt Kate was waiting at the door. Her hair, as white and fluffy as a dandelion clock, bristled with an assortment of hairclips. 'Come on in out of the rain, you boys!' she said, bundling them inside, smiling and dipping her head to look over her glasses. 'Now, I've made some of those jam tarts you like so much.'

Jack had a feeling Aunt Kate hadn't *totally* caught on to the twenty-first century yet. She seemed to think Dad had gone out to play thirty years ago and brought a couple of friends home for tea.

'Super!' Dad rubbed his hands together, as if a jam tart was the most exciting thing that had happened to him all year.

Then again, in Castle Key it probably *would* be.

The cottage was stuffed full of marmite-brown beams and flowery cushions. Jack sighed and helped himself to a jam tart. He tried to not think about what he'd be doing if he was at home: *meeting up at the BMX park with Josh and Ali, catching the new Batman film, going out for a pizza . . .*

It was so unfair!

―

After they'd said goodbye to Dad and finished dinner, Scott was at a loose end. Usually, he spent the evening having a kick-about with his mates, rehearsing with his band, The Banners, or playing computer games. He'd been planning to bring his laptop with him to Stone Cottage, but it had blown up the day before they left; it clearly didn't fancy spending the summer in Castle Key any more than he did! There *was* a computer at Stone Cottage – a hulking brontosaurus of a machine on the desk in the living room – but even if it had enough memory to load a game, which Scott doubted, it was strictly for Aunt Kate's work. She was an author, which wasn't as interesting as it sounded, since she only wrote *romantic* novels! There were games in the cupboard under the stairs, but a brief inspection revealed nothing more thrilling than Snakes and Ladders.

Scott switched on the TV. It was so small you practically needed a telescope, and there were only four channels. The most exciting programme all evening was a documentary about newts. He switched it off.

'Might as well go to bed!' Jack grumbled. Scott trudged after him. Every stair creaked. So did the floorboards and the door. Their bedroom was tucked under the sloping ceiling. Jack threw himself down on the nearest of the two high, narrow beds. 'I'm not staying here! We *have* to run away and get back to London! We can stay at Josh's house!'

Scott stood at the small window, picking out chords on his guitar while gazing out at the roses in the back garden, which were being pushed around by the wind and the rain. He turned to his brother and shook his head.

Jack sat up and thumped his pillow. His thick blond hair was sticking up like a cockatoo's crest and his eyes sparked with anger. 'Oh, so you're going to be all *mature* and Let's-Make-The-Best-Of-It, are you?'

Scott grabbed a rolled-up sock and aimed it at

his brother. He was only a year older than Jack, but sometimes it felt like decades. And it wasn't just that he was so much taller. Perhaps it was because he could still remember Mum, but Jack couldn't. She had died in a car crash when Scott was four. *A kiss goodnight, the smell of lemon soap, walking under the trees in a park somewhere;* as fragile as butterfly wings, Scott kept the memories locked up in a safe place. But just because he kept his cool and didn't rant and rave like Jack, didn't mean he *liked* having to spend his summer on The Isle of Nowhere. 'Dad made us promise we wouldn't cause Aunt Kate any trouble, remember?'

Jack snorted and fired the sock back at Scott. '*Trouble?* That's a joke! What kind of trouble could we get up to in this dump?'

Scott climbed into bed, under the geological layers of woollen blankets, and stared at the cracks in the ceiling. Jack was right. There was nothing to do here, no one to hang out with and nowhere to go.

This was going to be the worst summer ever!

Jack was woken by the smell of frying bacon. Sunlight was streaming in round the curtains. He hopped out of bed and gave Scott's comatose form a good shake. 'Come on, Sloth-features!' he shouted,' I'm starving!'

Aunt Kate smiled at them as she placed full cooked breakfasts on the kitchen table. *At least the food's good here,* Jack thought, tucking into bacon and scrambled eggs. Better than *good.* This was an *awesome breakfast!* At home, they just helped themselves to Coco Pops. Things were looking up. Maybe he wouldn't run away *just* yet.

Aunt Kate wiped her hands on her blue and white striped apron and lent back against the cooker – one of those big old-fashioned range-style things – nodding approvingly as she watched them eat. 'Dinner will be on the table at seven every day. I know you boys'll want to go off exploring, so I've made you packed lunches. I'm busy with my new book, but I'm sure you'll find plenty to do. Just try not to injure yourselves *too* badly. And don't get arrested!' Aunt Kate added with a smile. 'The hospital and the police station are both on the mainland in Carrickstowe, and I don't have a car.'

Arrested? Jack nearly choked on his fried bread. *That'd be a challenge in this place!*

Scott was obviously thinking the same thing, 'Arrested for what? Breathing in an Offensive Manner?' he whispered.

'Sneezing without Due Care and Attention?' Jack laughed.

Aunt Kate was too busy clattering about at the sink to hear them. 'Oh, and don't go wandering on the cliffs near the ruined castle,' she warned, 'It's very dangerous where the ground is crumbling away.'

Dangerous cliffs? Ruined castles? At last it sounded as if there might be *something* worth checking out in Castle Key.

'We'll stay well away,' Jack said.

With his fingers crossed firmly behind his back, of course.

Two

The Carrickstowe Hoard

Scott shouldered his backpack, let the garden gate swing shut behind him and followed Jack out into Church Lane. It was a sunny morning and Scott had to admit Stone Cottage looked much better than it had in last night's rain. And the garden looked like a screensaver or a picture on a calendar, with flowers spilling out over the path. But it was quiet. *Too* quiet! No cars or buses, no road works, no people rushing around with their take-out coffees and mobile phones. Just birds twittering at each other in the hedgerow.

'Maybe everyone's died of boredom!' Jack joked, pointing at the moss-covered gravestones crowding round the old stone church.

Soon they reached the bottom of the hill and turned into the high street. They mooched along, past a pub, a newsagent, and a shop that seemed to sell farming tools, fudge and ladies' slippers. They were all closed. But although there was no sign of intelligent life, Scott couldn't shake the spooky sensation that they were being watched. *Probably just that one-eyed tabby cat on the Post Office doorstep.* 'Welcome to the pulsating heart of Dullsville, Arizona! Watch out for low-flying tumbleweed!' he said.

Jack laughed. But not for long. 'It's too hot,' he complained. 'And I'm starving!'

'What's new?' Scott shook his head. Only *Jack* could be hungry half an hour after a full fried breakfast.

Jack ignored him. 'Let's find that "smashing" café Dad was on about and get an ice cream.'

The boys cut through Fish Alley and came out on the seafront. But when they reached Dotty's Tea Rooms, the red checked curtains were drawn and a sign on the door announced, *Sorry, We're Closed* in faded letters.

Jack rattled the door handle in frustration.

'Chill!' Scott said, 'We'll find somewhere else.'

Jack ground his teeth. He'd been really looking

forward to that ice cream! And there was nothing in the entire universe that annoyed him more than Scott doing that cool pose and telling him to chill! He marched off, scuffing up clouds of dust with every step.

'Where're you going?' Scott called after him.

'Nowhere!' Jack yelled.

Nowhere! He fumed. *That just about sums this place up*. And now there was a stupid wall in the way. He climbed over it and landed on a pebbly beach. He didn't stop until the water's edge, where foamy frills lapped at his trainers. A fossilised old man, wearing a woolly hat in spite of the heat, was sitting on a boat tied up against the harbour wall. He glanced up from what looked like *knitting* fishing nets or something, and nodded.

Jack picked up a stone and, with a flick of his wrist, launched it into the air. But it didn't skim and bounce across the water. It sank with a plop. *Typical!* Even the stones were rubbish in Castle Key!

But suddenly Jack remembered two things that cheered him up. Number One, there were sandwiches in the backpack. He wasn't going to starve, after all. And Number Two, didn't Aunt Kate mention *something* at breakfast this morning that sounded interesting? Oh yes! *The ruined castle on the dangerous cliffs!* Jack shaded his eyes and looked up. The cliffs towered up from the sea at the eastern end of the harbour, taller than high-rise blocks of flats. He turned to Scott, who'd followed him onto the beach, and pointed up at the jagged outline of the ruins on the cliff-top. 'Let's go up to the castle.'

'Sure,' Scott said casually.

Jack did a double take. Scott was usually a bit *picky* about doing really dangerous things they weren't allowed to do. 'It's going to be an epic climb!' Jack said, eying the sheer rock-faces again.

Scott laughed and gave Jack a shove. 'D'you think you're Spiderman or something? We're not going up the *cliffs*.

I should have known he'd bottle it! Jack thought.

But suddenly Scott took off at a run. 'There's a road up to the castle from the village. I saw it signposted,' he called over his shoulder, 'What are you waiting for?'

Jack raced to catch up with Scott. Trust his brother to have noticed something important like a road to the castle and not bother mentioning it.

Castle Road wound its way steeply up the hill. By the time the boys reached the top they were hot and tired.

'I hope it's worth it!' Jack groaned, trudging through a wrought-iron gate and across a small gravel parking area in front of the castle ruins. A signboard had been placed in the middle of the car park.

'CLOSED FOR BUILDING WORK!' Jack read.

'I don't believe it!' Scott slapped his palms to his forehead. He sank down on to a grassy bank that must once have been part of the moat. 'The only *remotely* cool place in a ten-mile radius and it's *shut*!'

Jack flopped down next to him and stared furiously at the ruins – as if they were personally responsible for the whole Disaster Zone that was Castle Key. There was no roof and only two of the four corner towers were still standing. Half the walls had avalanched into tumbling heaps of turrets, ramparts and random lumps of stone – all the same shortbread colour as the cliffs below. 'Building work!' he snorted. 'Yeah right!'

'Ha! Not the castle itself. The museum.' Jack looked up to see that the voice came from a man striding towards them across the car park. Wire-rimmed glasses were perched on his hooked nose and the waves of white hair swooping out from either side of his wide forehead gave him the look of a geriatric lion. He smiled and held out his hand. 'Geoff Piggott, Curator of Castle Museum.'

'Or, er, hello.' Scott scrambled to his feet and shook hands. 'I'm Scott and this is Jack. We're . . .'

'I know; you can't keep anything quiet for long round here. You're Leo Carter's boys. I'm familiar with your father's work in Africa, of course . . .'

Mr Piggott continued to ramble on as he led them round to the far side of the castle. Jack tuned out. People always thought that just because his Dad was into digging up old stuff, *he* was too. *Not!* They came to a modern building jutting out from the side of the castle.

'This is the museum,' Mr Piggott announced proudly.

'It was built in the 1980s, although the offices and storerooms are part of the original castle kitchens and cellars. We're installing a new security system ready for The Hoard.'

'The Hoard?' Jack echoed. Now this sounded more interesting! Like something out of *The Lord of the Rings*. He imagined an army of blood-crazed orcs storming the castle.

'The *Carrickstowe* Hoard,' Mr Piggott explained. 'Saxon treasure discovered just a few miles away. This island was once an important site for ritual burials, it seems. The Hoard is one of the most significant finds since Sutton Hoo. It's been on display at the British Museum, but they're lending us some of the artefacts for a special exhibition so they can be seen on their home ground, so to speak.' Mr Piggott beamed as if he'd just won Museum Curator of the Year. 'Now, I don't know how much you know about Saxon burials, but they're most unusual in Cornwall, where the Celts held out against the Saxons until . . .'

To Jack's relief, Mr Piggott's lecture was interrupted by the arrival of a little old lady on a bike. She was wearing a pink floral apron, an orange high-visibility waistcoat over her dress and trainers on her feet, and when she hopped down, her back was hunched – as if she were still leaning over the handlebars. She began hurling mops and brooms out of the small trailer attached to the back of the bike. *She cycled up that hill?* Jack marvelled.

And it's not even a mountain bike. Respect!

'I'll start in the foyer, Mr Piggott!' she shouted, removing her cycling helmet and patting her grey curls.

'Right you are,' the curator replied. Then he turned to the boys. 'Mrs Loveday's our caretaker.'

'And if that Pete Morley's got sawdust all over my skirting boards again, I'll have his Guts for Gargoyles!' Mrs Loveday added, with the ferocity of a wild tiger defending its territory. She stomped off towards the museum, dragging a vacuum cleaner across the gravel.

'Doesn't she mean guts for *garters?*' Scott whispered.

Jack grinned. The image of Mrs Loveday helping herself to someone's guts – whatever she was going to use them for – was a terrifying one. Given the option, he'd take the blood-crazed orcs any day!

'Mrs Loveday's the one who's *really* in charge up here, not me,' Mr Piggott chuckled, hooking his thumbs into the belt-loops of his baggy tweed trousers. 'Now, you two look as if you could do with an ice cream. I think there're some in the freezer in the museum shop.' He beckoned for the boys to follow him into the museum foyer and then disappeared through a side door.

Jack noticed a pile of posters on a desk in the corner and wandered over for a look. 'Wow, look at this bling!' he breathed, holding one up to show Scott. Filling the entire poster, beneath the words THE MARVELS OF THE CARRICKSTOWE HOARD AT CASTLE MUSEUM, was a photograph of the Saxon treasure: a glistening golden shield carved with wonderful beasts and intricate patterns, a helmet dripping with red and amber jewels, and, right in the middle, a mighty double-edged sword with a fabulously decorated hilt.

'Not bad,' Scott agreed, 'I wouldn't mind seeing that stuff.'

Mr Piggott returned moments later holding out two orange ice-lollies. 'On the house.' Then he saw that Jack was still holding up a poster. 'Ah yes, the exhibition opens next Thursday. I hope you'll come back then. The artefacts are even more spectacular in real life.'

For another mind-numbing monologue on Saxon funerals? Jack thought. *No thanks!* Then again, if there were free ice-lollies on offer again, it *might* be worth another visit. And that sword did look pretty cool. Although he didn't suppose they'd let him have a go with it . . .

Little did Jack know they'd be back at the castle well before next Thursday – and with something much more interesting than one of Mr Piggott's history lessons on the agenda.

Three

Not Your Average Girl

How come *everyone* in this place is *ancient*? Jack grumbled, his mouth bright orange from the ice-lolly, as they walked back down Castle Road.

'Yeah, it's spooky!' Scott agreed. 'Maybe they keep all the kids locked up as slaves?' He stuck his hands in his jeans pockets and continued walking in silence. *How on earth are we going to fill the rest of the summer?* he wondered.

'This looks like a short cut down to the village.' Jack was already climbing over a stile into a field of long grass when Scott noticed a herd of cows. Very big black and white cows, *looking at them*. 'Maybe we should just stick to the road,' he said. 'They might be bulls.'

'Bulls!' Jack snorted. 'Bulls have horns and rings through their noses.'

Scott hesitated.

'Come on, you wuss!' Jack laughed.

'I. Am. Not. A. Wuss!' Scott protested. He was well known for being one of the toughest defenders on his football team and he never shied away from a hard tackle. He just liked to take a chilled approach to life. He didn't see the point of taking stupid risks. Unlike Jack! As far as Jack was concerned, the stupider the better. And right now he was skipping along the path like a demented Easter Bunny. Scott had no choice but to follow him.

He kept a careful eye on the cows. Worryingly, they were starting to toss their heads around and blow through their noses. Scott quickened his step.

Suddenly he heard the pounding of hooves. Hundreds of man-eating bulls were stampeding towards them! His heart nearly beating out of his chest, Scott accelerated to a sprint. Ahead of him, Jack turned, took one look and also started to run.

Scott could feel hot, damp breath on his neck. Any second now he was going to be gored through the heart. *We're going to die!* He closed his eyes and braced himself for impact. But it didn't come. He opened his eyes again and the first thing he saw was a little brown and white shaggy dog racing around in the grass. Then he saw a girl. 'Run!' Scott shouted, grabbing hold of her arm. *'Bulls!'*

But the girl pulled away. She clapped her hands and stamped a bare, brown foot. 'Shoo!' she yelled. Then she threw her head back and laughed. It was a surprisingly loud laugh, like an orchestra of violins tuning up. 'They're not bulls. Just cheeky young heifers.' She stamped her foot again. The cows lowered their heads and ambled away towards a patch of thistles.

'Yeah, I thought so,' Scott panted, trying to catch his breath and regain some dignity. 'We just didn't want to take any chances.'

Jack flopped down on the grass. The little dog – who looked like a cross between a spaniel, a Jack Russell and a teddy bear – started bouncing around on top of him as if he were a human trampoline. Jack laughed. 'You should have seen your face, Scotto! I *told* you they weren't bulls.'

'Excuse me, *you* were legging it too,' Scott pointed out.

The girl sat down next to Jack. 'Don't they *have* cows in London?'

'Yeah, can't move for them!' Scott snapped. And then, because the fright was wearing off and he couldn't resist the joke, '*Moo*-ching around on street corners!'

The girl did that laugh again.

'Er, how did you know we're from London?' Jack asked.

'Been tailing you all morning. I've been working on my Undercover Surveillance techniques and I'm getting pretty good, if I say so myself.'

'Oh yeah?' Scott said, 'Nothing ever happens In Castle Key. What could you possibly have to *survale*?' He realized too late that there was no such word as *survale*. Luckily the girl didn't seem to notice.

'Ah, that's what you think,' she said. 'It's a *bit* quiet this morning because it's Sunday, but . . .' she glanced over her shoulder and lowered her voice, 'there's all sorts of *highly suspicious goings-on*. Mr McElroy is running a spy ring from the Post Office, and there's an illegal gambling den at Dotty's on Friday nights . . .'

Scott shrugged. This girl was obviously a total nutcase, but she seemed harmless enough. And at least now he knew who'd been watching them on the high street!

'I'm Emily Wild,' the girl announced. Scott could see now that she was older than he'd thought; about the same age as Jack. She was wearing an old white t-shirt and denim shorts. Her eyes were so dark they were almost black and her small chin was pointed. There was something elf-like about her. Scott wondered whether she had pointed ears too, but they were hidden beneath a long tangle of conker-brown curls – which probably accounted for about half her bodyweight. 'And this is Drift.' She ruffled the little dog's fur. 'We live in The Lighthouse.'

'Lighthouse?' Scott echoed.

'Yeah, you know, out in the bay?' Emily shook her head and laughed. 'So you didn't *notice* the tall red and white striped building with the big light on top? Halfway along the promontory that sticks out from the end of the harbour? You two aren't exactly spy material are you?'

'So is your dad like the lighthouse keeper or something?' Jack's imagination was conjuring up thrilling images of storms and smugglers and shipwrecks.

'No. Mum and Dad run it as a Bed and Breakfast. It means they're really busy in the holidays so I have to do my own thing. But some of the guests are interesting. We get a lot of international criminals on the run, people leading double lives . . .' Emily jumped up and brushed grass seeds off her legs. 'Let's go down to the river. There's a really cool rope swing.' With that, she hared off across the meadow, Drift bounding along at her heels.

'Come on,' Jack said, starting to sprint after her.

Scott hesitated. Then he gave a *why not* shrug. 'Well, at least she's not *ancient*!'

When they caught up with Emily she was already swinging on a rope hanging from the branch of a willow tree. She soared in a perfect arc and landed with a splash. 'Wow!' Jack laughed, pulling off his shoes and socks. 'That looks awesome.' Moments later he was shouting *Geronimo-o-o-o-o* and plunging into the sub-zero water. 'Come on, Scott,' he called, gasping for air as he surfaced, 'your turn.'

Scott gave the rope a little tug. Jack could tell he was carrying out one of his personal health-and-safety inspections. It must have passed, because suddenly Scott was landing almost on top of him.

When they were tired of hurling themselves into the river, they lay on the bank to dry off. 'Yes, I *know* you're hungry,' Emily mumbled. 'I've got some treats for you.'

Jack stared at her. Yes, it was true, he *was* starving, but he hadn't said a word. He'd already figured out Emily wasn't exactly your *average* girl, but was she a mind-reader too?

'I was talking to Drift,' Emily laughed. 'He communicates with his ears.'

One of the little dog's ears – the black one – was flopped across his eye. The other, which was white with brown spots, was standing up straight.

'If I do that with *my* ears, can I have a treat too?' Jack joked.

'No need,' Scott laughed, reaching for the backpack. 'We've got packed lunches, remember?'

Jack fell on the sandwiches like a vulture.

'D'you want one before Jack inhales them all?' Scott asked Emily.

Emily took a mobile phone from her shoulder-bag and checked the time. 'Sorry, got to run! Business to attend to. But I'll take you to the Whistling Caves tomorrow if you like.'

'Whistling Caves?' Jack repeated. 'As in . . .' He pursed up his lips and shrilled a piercing wolf-whistle.

Emily grinned. 'Something like that, yeah. They're in the cliffs on the other side of Lighthouse Point.'

'Well,' Scott joked, 'we'll have to check our social diaries first, but I think we can squeeze it in.'

But Emily had already gone.

Jack lay back and let the sunshine filtering through the willow leaves warm his face. OK, the Bull Run Episode had been a bit hairy – not that he'd ever admit it, of course – but that was the best rope swing ever, and caves that whistled? That sounded *awesome!*

Castle Key had certainly got a lot more interesting since Emily and Drift had turned up.

Four

A Surprise at the Whistling Caves

E mily and Drift perched on a rock in the little inlet between the lighthouse and the harbour where she moored her rowing boat, *Gemini,* and waited for Scott and Jack. She'd already had a busy morning on a stake-out at the Post Office; she was sure Mr McElroy was passing on coded messages to selected customers, but after an hour lurking behind the greetings cards she still had nothing concrete to go on. She took out her phone and logged the series of photographs she'd taken earlier. You never knew when some seemingly innocent detail would turn out to be a vital clue.

Emily was looking forward to seeing the boys again. Jack was fun, if a bit crazy, and the older one, Scott, was cool. He just needed to lighten up a bit. Emily didn't really mind spending the days on her own – she was used to it – and she was never really on her own with Drift, of course. But it would be good to have some *human* company. Her friends from school were away on holiday or lived miles away on the mainland.

Emily peered through her binoculars. She could scope out the entire harbour from this vantage point. She noted three boats returning from overnight fishing trips, a cat stealing from a litter bin, and two men leaving Dotty's with take-away coffees. She recognized them as the security guards looking after the Carrickstowe Hoard up at the castle. At last, the boys came into view along the seafront. Scott was the shape of a question mark with his loping, slouchy walk, whereas Jack was tacking back and forth, kicking stones, banging a stick on the railing, elbowing Scott in the ribs. Drift shot off across the beach to meet them, tail wagging like a propeller. He clearly approved, which meant they *had* to be OK. Drift was an excellent judge of character.

'Come on,' Emily urged, waving at them. 'The caves are in the cliffs below the castle but we have to row all the way round Lighthouse Point to the other side of the bay to get to them.' She slipped the bowline from the mooring ring and began to tug *Gemini* across the shingle. Scott helped guide the boat into the shallow water.

Jack stared. 'We're going by boat?'

Emily laughed. 'Well spotted! It's far too steep to climb over the promontory. What's the matter? You can swim, can't you?'

'Of course, I can,' Jack fired back. It was true. He *could* swim. Just not with any style or skill. Scott, on the other hand, could torpedo through the water like a shark with a train to catch. 'I can't wait to hear this whistling,' he said, in a hasty bid to change the subject, casually chucking his socks and trainers into the boat.

'I expect it's just a bit of low-level murmuring,' Scott said, 'You know, like wind in the telegraph wires or something.'

And when did Scott suddenly become a world expert on the sound effects of caves? Jack wondered.

'Ah, you wait and see, laddie.'

Jack whipped round and came face to face with the old guy he'd seen at the harbour yesterday. His skin was as brown and cracked as an old leather suitcase and he was still wearing the woolly hat. He laughed and winked at Emily.

'I'm just back from fishing round the other side. Caves are on top form!' He turned and squinted up at the castle ruins on the cliff-top, then nodded – so slowly Jack thought he'd fallen asleep. Suddenly he re-booted. 'There's an old saying in the village . . . *When the whistling do cease, the castle shall know no peace*!'

'Wow! You mean the castle will be attacked or something?' Jack breathed, 'Has it ever happened?'

'Not since 1385,' the old man chuckled. 'Off you go now. You'll be safe with young Emily.'

'That's Old Bob,' Emily said, once they were all aboard. She gripped the oars and began to pull away from the shore. 'He's been a fisherman in Castle Key since . . .'

'. . . 1385?' Jack joked.

'Yeah, nearly!' Emily laughed.

Jack settled down on the wooden seat and looked around. Sunlight was sparkling on the sea like sequins. Drift had taken up position at the front of the boat – the *bow* as Emily called it – and stood with his front paws on the side, his ears blowing back in the wind. On their left the promontory pointed out to sea like a giant craggy finger. It was nowhere near as high as the cliffs, of course, but the rocks were steep and sheer. It would be an awesome place to climb. Climbing was much more Jack's scene than swimming.

'Do you want to row for a while?' Emily asked.

'Sure,' Jack had never rowed a boat before but it didn't look as if there was much to it. A bit of wood in each hand. *How hard can it be?* Emily showed him how to hold the oars. He braced and pulled with all his strength. One oar flew out of the water and almost whacked Scott on the head. The other refused to budge. Suddenly they were spinning round in circles.

'We're not on the dodgems you know,' Scott laughed.

Jack tried again. After a while he got the hang of it. At least they were moving in the right direction, but his arms soon started to ache. Then Scott had a go. To Jack's delight, Scott was even worse at rowing than he was, and Emily took over again as they neared the end of the promontory and began weaving among the rocks that jutted up like broken teeth. At last they rounded the final outcrop and came out into the other side of the bay.

Emily pointed at the cliffs. 'There! Can you see the caves? Below the castle?'

Scott laughed. He knew Emily didn't exactly rate his powers of observation, but you'd have to be wearing a blindfold not to see the caves. The entire cliff-face was peppered with hollows and crevices – like mouths gaping in horror and vacant black eye sockets. And where the wall of rock plunged into the sea, the waves had carved out a series of caverns, complete with pillars and arches. He had to admit, it *was* pretty impressive.

'Awesome!' Jack sighed.

'Shhh,' Emily put her finger to her lips. 'We'll hear the whistling any second now. 'Listen.'

Scott listened. He listened to the cries of the seagulls wheeling overhead. He listened to the crash and smack of the waves, the creak of the oars against the side of the boat.

There was no whistling.

Jack cupped his hands behind his ears as if that would help.

'Must be the wind direction or something.' Emily snatched the oars up and rowed inland until they were almost in the shadow of the cliffs.

There was still no whistling.

Five

Missing

W *histling caves!* Scott thought. *Yeah, right!* Even though he'd *known* caves couldn't really whistle, he still felt a pang of disappointment.

'What *kind* of whistling is it, exactly?' Jack asked in a helpful tone. 'Is it like a referee blowing for half-time or more of a low hum, you know, like a vuvuzela or something?'

But Emily just shook her head and slumped over

the oars. Her hair dangled over her knees and trailed in the water at the bottom of the boat. 'But they were whistling earlier this morning when Old Bob was here,' she muttered. 'This has never happened before.'

'Well, not since 1385!' Jack laughed.

But Emily wasn't laughing. She looked as if she was about to cry. Drift whimpered and pawed at her leg, his ears drooping.

Scott couldn't help feeling sorry for her. He'd been about to start whistling the theme tune from *Match of the Day* as a joke. But he decided against it. He suddenly realized he *liked* Emily. Yes, she was a bit like James Bond's annoying little sister, but she was OK. Back home, his mates would all tease him and say he *fancied* her, of course, but that's not what he meant. Emily wasn't like other girls. In fact, she wasn't like *anyone* else. 'Never mind, Em,' he offered. 'They're still pretty cool caves.'

Emily thanked him with a fragile smile.

'Ooh, I think I'm getting something,' Jack cried. 'No, sorry, false alarm. Just a seagull.'

'Let's go,' Emily said in a small, flat voice, digging the right oar hard into the water to turn the boat around.

By the time they were tethering the little boat back to the mooring ring half an hour later, Jack had already forgotten about the caves. He was hot and thirsty. And he was very hungry. So when Emily suggested that they go up to The Lighthouse for lunch, it took him less than a nanosecond to agree.

'Mum usually does a buffet for the guests,' she said, leading the way up a steep flight of steps, hewn into the rocks, and towards the end of the promontory along a path that must have been crafted by kamikaze mountain goats. Jack climbed eagerly, spurred on by the magical word *buffet,* and its promise of cold roast chicken and sausage rolls, pavlova and trifle . . .

Up close, The Lighthouse – which looked like a little red and white Lego tower from the sea – was a surprisingly solid building that seemed to grow right out of the rock. A heavy wooden door opened into a huge circular room, crammed with sofas, rugs and lamps. The curved walls were smothered with bright wall hangings and paintings. It was like walking inside a giant kaleidoscope. In the middle of it all was a spiral staircase. Jack craned his neck and looked up. The staircase went up so far it made him dizzy.

'There are nine floors,' Emily said. 'This is the guest lounge and reception. The kitchen is the next floor up, then the three guest rooms have a floor each, then our family living room, Mum and Dad's room, and our bathroom. My room is right at the top, under the Lantern Room. I've got a three hundred and sixty degree view.'

'Wow!' Jack sighed. 'Having the penthouse suite in a lighthouse. How cool is that?'

'It can be a bit noisy in a storm!' Emily laughed. 'And it's really annoying if I forget to bring something down from my room. It's one hundred and twenty steps to go back up! But apart from that I love it.'

Jack grinned, happy that Emily had cheered up after the Non-Whistling Caves Episode. Being miserable didn't suit her. *Now, where's that buffet . . .*

Emily led them through to a sunny conservatory that had been added to the side of the guest lounge. The panoramic view of cliffs and ocean and sky was breathtaking. *Not as breathtaking as the view of the buffet table, though,* Jack thought. OK, there were no whole roast chickens, but he was prepared to overlook that, given the presence of home-made pork pies, Cornish pasties, baked potatoes, hams and Spanish tapas, not to mention the selection of cakes at the other end of the table. Castle Key was definitely starting to grow on him.

He was beginning to tuck in when a woman in a purple tie-dye dress, her long dark hair wound up in a tasseled scarf, swept down the stairs. She raised her hands in a kind of long-distance high-five. 'Hey kids! *Hola.* Welcome to The Lighthouse. Help yourselves.' With that, she scooped up a pile of sheets from a chair and wafted up the stairs again.

'Mum's from Spain,' Emily said, 'and she's an artist,' she added, as if that explained everything.

Just as Mrs Wild left, the front door flew open and a

tall man wandered in. 'Hey, Emski, you seen my pliers? Tap's leaking in Room Two again.' He stopped when he saw the boys and held up a hand. 'Hey there, nice to meet you.' Then he wandered off to the other side of the dining room still searching for the pliers.

Scott thought there was something familiar about Mr Wild. He'd definitely seen him before somewhere; the long grey hair tied in a thin ponytail, the hooked nose, the deep-set blue eyes. Of course, he was *Seth Wild!* He only used to be the guitarist with Panic Mode. Wow! How cool was that? Not that Scott was into eighties rock in a big way, but before he retired from the music business, Seth Wild was one of the greatest guitar legends ever . . .

'You didn't tell me your Dad was Seth Wild,' Scott whispered.

'You didn't ask,' Emily replied with a grin. Then she turned to her father. 'Dad, something really strange just happened. The Whistling Caves have stopped whistling.'

'Ha ha, very funny. You have to watch my daughter, boys. She has a very active imagination!'

'It's true,' Jack said, his mouth full of Cornish pasty. 'We didn't hear a thing!'

'I thought you kids were meant to have better hearing than us old-timers,' Seth laughed, cruising past the buffet table and snagging a handful of olives. 'Those caves make a *ser-i-ous* racket. Even *I* can hear them and

43

I've played a few *loud* concerts in my time.'

Emily shrugged. 'So no one believes me. What's new?'

'*We* believe you, don't we, Scott? ' Jack elbowed his brother hard in the ribs.

'Er, yeah, of course,' Scott muttered.

'Come on then.' Emily was already on her way out of the door with Drift at her heels. 'We need to find Old Bob. He'll know what to do about it.'

'Won't he be out fishing again?' Jack asked.

Emily shook her head. 'Not on a Monday lunchtime. He'll be at Dotty's with a bowl of tomato soup and a mug of tea.'

—

Unlike yesterday the café was bustling with life. And, just as Emily had predicted, Old Bob was at a window table dipping bread into his tomato soup.

Jack's mental image of someone called Dotty had curlers and a zimmer frame, but to his surprise the woman behind the counter was young and pretty, in a *Hannah Montana* kind of way, wearing a low-cut dress with a pink polka dot pattern – not that he noticed such things of course. Right now, he was more interested in the cakes. Emily had dragged him away from The Lighthouse before he'd been able to sample the selection there.

'Ah! Smashing!' he said, rubbing his hands together and mimicking Dad's enthusiastic tone.

'Smashing!' Scott fired back, laughing.

'Er, *smashing*?' Emily asked. 'Is that some kind of cool London slang I should know about?'

Jack laughed. 'Just a family joke!' He returned to the important business of selecting the largest chocolate fudge muffin. Which would need a Coke to wash it down, of course.

They took their trays and sat down at the next table to Old Bob. He slurped his tea and nodded a greeting.

'Something's gone wrong with the caves. They've stopped whistling,' Emily whispered urgently.

But before Old Bob could reply, the door banged open and a little old lady shot in as if she'd been fired from a cannon. Jack was sure he'd seen her somewhere before. Oh yes, that was it; the caretaker from up at the castle, the one with sawdust on her skirting boards. Mrs Lovebird or something.

'Oooh! I'm all a-flutter!' she announced to the room in general. 'I think I'm having a Nervous Breakdance. There's been a terrible to-do up at the castle.'

Suddenly Jack remembered Old Bob's saying. Something about the castle being attacked if the caves stop whistling. *Had it come true?* A chill trickled down his spine – and it wasn't just from the Coke that had gone down the wrong way! Then he shook himself. This was real life, not a computer game! *Who attacks castles these days? William the Conqueror? Genghis Khan?*

The café had fallen silent. All eyes were on Mrs Loveday. She patted her chest as if to jump-start her heart and puffed out her cheeks. Dotty came round from behind the counter and took her arm, but Mrs Loveday waved her away. 'It's the Carrickstowe Hoard! The Chieftain's Shield has gone missing!'

There was a sudden whoosh as steam spurted from the cappuccino machine.

'Missing?' Dotty echoed.

Mrs Loveday nodded importantly. '*Stolen!* Right out from under our noses.'

'*When the whistling do cease . . .*' Old Bob murmured into his mug of tea.

'*The castle shall know no peace . . .*' Emily breathed.

Maybe, just maybe, Jack thought, *something* exciting *has actually happened in Castle Key!*

Six

The Windmill of Opportunity

Emily gripped the arms of her chair, her heart doing backflips with excitement. This was just the kind of major investigation she'd been waiting for. Operation Post Office would have to be put on hold with immediate effect. She thought about whether she should let the boys in on the case. She usually worked alone – you could slip under cover more easily that way – but with a bit of training Scott and Jack could be useful. And from the looks on their faces they were as enthralled as she was.

Mrs Loveday and her nerves were now ensconced at a corner table, being treated for shock with a cup of tea and a jam doughnut.

'Come on!' Emily hissed. 'We've got work to do!

They took the short cut through the cow field up to the castle and arrived less than twenty minutes later. Emily picked out the densest holly bush at the edge of the car park as the perfect Observation Post. 'Stake-out!' she commanded. Drift instantly froze and lay down next to her. They all peeped out through the leaves. A quick scan of the location revealed orange crime-scene tape across the entrance to the museum and a police vehicle in the car park. From the registration number, Emily knew that Detective Inspector Hassan was on the scene already.

Then she noticed the two security guards. They were leaning against the bonnet of their van in the car park swigging from cans of Coke. One was tall and brown-skinned and looked as if he spent a lot of time lifting weights. The other was plump with wiry red hair and freckles.

'You didn't tell anyone the code for the safe, did you?' Freckle Guy asked.

'D'you think I'm stupid or something?' Muscle Man snapped.

'Keep your hair on, mate!' Freckle Guy crushed his

Coke can. 'You know the police are going to ask us this stuff. We need to make sure we've done everything by the book . . . '

'Well, we have, haven't we? Everything was present and correct when we did our routine tour of the storeroom at ten. Then we checked the main safe at midday, and the shield had vanished into thin air. End of story.'

The guards fell silent and Emily's attention switched to a young woman in a smart blue dress and high heels coming out of the museum. She recognised Victoria White, who lived at Roshendra Farm, not far from Castle Key. Vicky had helped out at The Lighthouse during summer seasons in the past, when she was home from university, but this year she was working for Mr Piggott on the publicity for the new exhibition. 'The police want to see you two now!' she shouted to the guards. Then she drove off in a red mini with a Union Jack painted on top.

The guards headed off towards the museum.

Emily took out her notebook, started a new section and wrote *Location of Theft: Main Safe In Storeroom. Time of Theft: 10.15 a.m. to 12 noon.*

Jack peered over her shoulder. 'You've put the wrong time. The guards said they checked at 10 o'clock, not 10.15.'

Emily grinned. 'First rule of investigation: don't believe *everything* people say. They may have been *meant* to do the check at ten. But I spotted them leaving Dotty's café with their coffees at 10.03 precisely. It takes at least twelve minutes to drive back up to the castle, so the theft must have taken place after 10.15.'

'Elementary, my dear Watson,' Scott laughed, brushing holly leaves from his jeans. 'So, while we were rowing round in circles listening to the Whistling Caves doing their world-famous *not-whistling* act, *someone* was up at the castle helping themselves to the Saxon treasure.'

'Looks that way,' Emily agreed, bouncing her pencil up and down on the notebook. Suddenly there was a crunching of tyres on gravel and they all leapt back behind the bush. Scott yelped as holly leaves prickled his arms. A bike was speeding into the car park.

'It's Mrs Lovely-Jubbly again,' Jack whispered.

'Perfect! Mrs Loveday is one of my best informants,' Emily said. 'OK, look *casual*.' With that, she popped out of the bush and ambled across the car park. Scott, Jack and Drift followed. Scott couldn't help grinning at Jack's Casual Pose, which consisted of sticking his hands in his pockets, looking at the sky and whistling tunelessly. He had *I've been up to something* written all over his face! In fact, if the police saw Jack right now they'd probably arrest him for stealing the Chieftain's Shield.

'Hello, Mrs Loveday,' Emily said in a voice as sweet as golden syrup. 'Surely you've not had to come back to work already after the shock you've had?'

'Oh, hello Emily, dear,' Mrs Loveday puffed as she bustled round to her trailer. 'The police will be wanting to talk to me. I'm a Principal Witness, you see. I was on the premises when the shield was stolen – during the Windmill of Opportunity.'

'You mean the *window* of opportunity?' Scott asked.

'Yes, that as well, dear.'

'I'm sure you'll have a lot to tell them?' Emily went on.

'Well, I'm not one to gossip, of course . . . ' Mrs Loveday's words resonated from the depths of the trailer – which had almost swallowed her up as she reached in for a huge box of paper towels.

Scott smiled. He'd heard that phrase before. Their next-door neighbour in London always said the same thing – just before she dished the dirt on the entire street! 'Let me help you with that,' he said politely, taking the box.

Mrs Loveday beamed at him. 'What a helpful young man!'

Works every time, Scott thought, handing the box to Jack so quickly he didn't have time to protest. 'You could probably tell the police a thing or two about what goes on at the castle,' he said.

'Oh yes!' Mrs Loveday gave a dark chuckle as if there were *certain* things she knew that would shock him to the core. 'I can't *abide* tittle-tattle, but the truth will out.

That Pete Morley – calls himself a *carpenter* – well, he's been in and out of prison, you know. Mr Piggott's too kind-hearted for his own good, taking on a Criminal Elephant like that!'

Criminal elephant? She must mean criminal element*!* Scott thought, disguising a snort of laughter as a sympathetic noise. Mrs Loveday lowered her voice to a stage whisper. 'And that Victoria White's no better than she should be! Right little flibbertigibbet, distracting the men from their work with her Feminist Wiles.'

'What about Piggott?' Jack piped up from behind the box of paper towels.

Mrs Loveday stopped in her tracks and stared at Jack, her eyes popping with horror – as if he'd suggested that the Pope himself could've broken in and pinched the shield. '*Mr Piggott* was working in his office all morning, I'll have you know. He was on the phone making *very* important calls. Not that I was ear-wigging of course but I couldn't help hearing while I was polishing the doorknobs in the corridor.'

For two hours? Emily thought. *Those doorknobs must be worn to stumps!* 'Oh, of course not!' she said in her most soothing voice. 'And was anyone else at the castle this morning?'

'Only little old me!' Mrs Loveday laughed, 'But what would *I* want with a Chieftain's Shield? I've no room on my mantelpiece what with all Norman's golf trophies.' She was still laughing as the museum door opened. Detective Inspector Hassan stepped out, filling the doorway like a grizzly bear in an immaculate dove-grey suit. When he spoke, his voice boomed out from beneath a luxuriant black moustache.

'We're ready for you now, Mrs Loveday.' Then he noticed Emily. 'I do hope you've not been bothering Mrs Loveday with questions about the theft?' The moustache appeared to be smiling but there was a gruff, no-nonsense edge to the words. 'This is far too serious an investigation for children to be mixed up in.'

Emily did her best to look innocent – although she was tempted to remind D. I. Hassan that without her investigative skills, he'd *still* be looking for the scrap-dealer who'd dumped old fridges on Westward Beach, not to mention the man who'd sabotaged the hanging baskets outside The Ship and Anchor.

'Don't you worry, Inspector Hasseem,' Mrs Loveday said, craning her neck to look up at the giant police officer. 'They haven't heard anything from me. Mum's the word!' With that she turned to Scott. 'Thank you for your help, dear.' She took the box of paper towels from Jack's arms and hoisted it onto her hip.

'Don't mention it!' Jack muttered under his breath.

Seven

Prime Suspects

Emily led the way to the farthest corner of the castle – under a ruined archway, down a flight of crumbling steps, and through a small hole in the wall to a secret room within a circular tower. OK, so the castle *was* officially closed at the moment, but she'd been using this hide-out for years, and they weren't doing any harm. She pulled out a packet of biscuits she'd squirrelled away in a little gap in the stonework under the shelter of a fallen plinth and sat down with her notebook at a desk she'd constructed from fallen stones.

Jack gave Scott an irritable shove. 'Next time you do your Helpful Young Man act, carry your *own* boxes. I thought my arms were going to drop off.'

Scott returned the shove with a little extra for good measure. 'I was just giving you something useful to do. I was busy interviewing a witness.'

'More like being a creepy suck-up! *Ooh, Mrs Loveday, let me help you with that,*' Jack fluted, gearing up for Round Two.

'Stop arguing!' Emily shouted. 'I'm trying to concentrate. We've got a crime to solve, remember?'

Jack broke off hostilities with Scott, helped himself to a custard cream, and looked around for the first time. *What a brilliant hide-out!* Arrow slits in the walls meant they could look out in all directions. The roof of the tower was open to the sky, which was as blue as a Chelsea shirt and alive with dive-bombing seagulls. Shafts of sunlight shone like laser beams through the honeycomb of cracks and crevices in the walls.

Jack grinned. Somehow, while he wasn't looking, Castle Key had stopped being the Most Boring Place on the Planet! He couldn't think of anywhere he'd rather be. Well, perhaps riding on *Oblivion* at Alton Towers or in the X-Games BMX Finals, but *apart* from that. Tracking down the Saxon Thief was exciting. Who could have taken that shield? Or, to use Mrs Loveday's phrase, who was the *Criminal Elephant*? Suddenly he was doubled over with laughter. 'The Criminal Elephant!' he squeaked, hardly able to breathe.

'And who had the *Windmill of Opportunity*?' Emily giggled. Now all three of them were shaking with laughter. Drift dashed around wagging his tail to show he thought it was funny too. When, at last, they recovered enough to speak, they gathered around Emily's rock desk and studied her notes. She had written *Prime Suspects* at the top of the page, and underlined it three times. Beneath the heading was a list of names.

1. Pete Morley
2. Victoria White
3. Mr Piggott
4. Mrs Loveday
5. Security Guard 1 (Freckles)
6. Security Guard 2 (Muscles)

'Only those six?' Jack asked.

'I'm sure Mrs Loveday would have noticed any other visitors,' Scott pointed out.

'And we have to start with the people we *know* were here this morning,' Emily said, 'and eliminate them one by one.'

'*E-lim-i-nate!*' Jack chanted, jumping up and pretending to spray machine gun fire around the room.

'Eliminate *from our enquiries*, I meant,' Emily laughed.

'I was joking,' Jack said, aiming his imaginary gun through an arrow slit. He was greeted with a sudden view of the vertical cliff-face plunging to the waves crashing over the rocks hundreds of feet below. One thing was certain; there was no way anyone could climb up to the castle from the sea.

Emily pulled her watch out of her bag. 'I've got to get home and help Mum with the dinner. 'Let's make a plan.'

Dinner? Jack thought. *That sounds like my kind of plan!*

'Yes, we need a plan,' Scott announced, as if it had been his idea.

'We need to follow up each suspect,' Emily said. 'Find out who had a motive.'

'That's easy,' Jack laughed. 'Who *hasn't* got a motive? That shield must be worth millions. You could see from the photo on the poster that it's huge and it's got gold and stuff all over it.'

Scott gave him one of those knowledgeable *don't-be-such-a-dork* looks that drove Jack crazy. 'It's not that simple,' he sighed, 'You'd have to *really* need the money to risk stealing something so famous, *and* you'd need to know how to find a buyer. It's not like you could just put it on eBay! *One priceless Saxon Shield; well-used but in good condition.*'

'And we need to check the suspects' alibis for this

morning,' Emily went on. 'Who had a chance to go into the storeroom alone?' She looked down at her list. 'Let's leave the security guards for now. I know Vicky White. I'll interview her. And I know where Mrs Loveday lives, so I can track her movements too.'

'Excellent,' Scott said. 'You take those two. Jack and I will investigate Pete Morley and Geoff Piggott.'

Jack looked at his brother. Was he serious? How were they going to investigate two suspects they didn't even know without Emily's expertise?'

'I can work on my own,' Scott said, 'if this is all a bit *difficult* for you.'

'And I can help after I've finished the other two,' Emily offered kindly.

Jack clenched his teeth. It *wasn't* too difficult and he *didn't* need help. Well, actually it *was* and he *did* – but that wasn't the point. He was just as capable of investigating as Scott was. He shrugged with what he hoped was an air of unruffled confidence. 'No problem. Just leave it with us.'

Emily smiled and took her mobile phone from her bag. 'Good. Let's swap numbers. We can call each other tomorrow for a progress report, say at midday.'

—

Aunt Kate placed a lasagne big enough for a family of eight body-builders, and a basket of garlic bread on the kitchen table. 'Did you have a good day, boys?' she asked.

Scott ladled lasagne onto his plate and considered. Since breakfast, he'd rowed round in circles, listened to some caves that didn't whistle, hidden in a holly bush and helped a gossipy old lady carry a box of paper towels. He'd not practised his guitar or played a computer game all day.

On paper, these were *not* the ingredients of a 'good' day at all.

'Awesome, thanks,' Jack mumbled, as he licked dripping butter from his garlic bread.

Scott grinned. Jack was right. It *had* been awesome. And he wasn't just talking about meeting Seth Wild.

The *only* problem was that he'd promised Emily that he and Jack would conduct an in-depth investigation into Pete Morley *and* Mr Piggott by lunchtime tomorrow. He'd made out he knew what he was doing, but, in fact, he didn't have a clue how to go about it. He was going to have to think fast.

There was no way he was phoning Emily tomorrow without *some* progress to report!

Eight

Background Research

'So, what's the plan?' Jack asked, barging into the bathroom the next morning.

Scott spat toothpaste into the basin and glared at Jack's reflection in the mirror. His little brother didn't seem to have grasped the basic concept of personal space yet.

It was so frustrating! Scott had been hoping that the spirit of Sherlock Holmes would visit him in his dreams, equipped with top tips for the Morley/Piggott investigation, but sadly the only nocturnal visitation had been *Jack* jumping on his bed with his so-called *Killer Ideas*. These mainly involved abseiling in through Pete Morley's bedroom window and planting bugging devices. Scott had been quick to point out the flaws in these schemes: not actually *having* any bugging devices, for a start. Not to mention any idea where Pete Morley's house was.

Scott had come up with one idea, although it was far from *killer*. In fact it was pretty lame. 'We'll look them up on the internet,' he said, 'Mr Piggott is into archaeology. We could see if he's published anything about Saxon treasure. And Mrs Loveday said Pete Morley had been in prison. Maybe we can find out what sort of crimes he committed from old newspaper reports . . .'

Jack's reflection wrinkled its nose. 'And how's any of *that* going to tell us if they nicked the shield?'

'It's *background research*!' Scott said, hoping that giving it a label would make it sound more impressive. 'Do you have any better ideas? That *don't* require us to wear Superman capes, that is?'

Jack shrugged. 'OK, we'll try it your way.'

Aunt Kate was busy working on her computer which meant there was no chance of borrowing it to get onto the internet. So after breakfast the boys set off, armed only with their sandwiches and Aunt Kate's library card. Castle Key Library, on the corner of the High Street and Fish Alley, was empty.

'My bookshelf at home is bigger than this!' Jack whispered, as they settled down at the two public computers at the back of the tiny room.

Scott laughed. At least the computers were state-of-the-art, with huge screens and high-speed internet connections. *What more could I want?* Scott sighed happily as his hand closed over the mouse and he began to click through menus. He'd missed his computer.

'Bags I do Morley,' Jack whispered. 'Prison is way more interesting than archaeology!'

Scott typed GEOFF PIGGOTT into the search engine and watched as results scrolled onto the screen. It appeared that Geoffrey Brian Piggott had been the curator of Castle Key museum for twenty years. He'd written several articles about Saxon archaeology, as well as two books about the history of the Carrickstowe area. Disappointingly, the search didn't reveal anything suspicious; there was nothing to hint that Geoff Piggott might have graduated from *studying* Saxon history to *stealing* it!

'Any luck?' he asked, leaning over Jack's shoulder.

'Put it this way,' Jack laughed, 'I don't think our Pete won the school prize for good behaviour!'

On the screen was a newspaper report from *The Carrickstowe Times*, July 1990:

RIDE IS OVER FOR LOCAL TEARAWAY

Peter Morley of Castle Key was sentenced to eighteen months in Youth Detention for taking a vehicle without consent and dangerous driving.

'Joy riding?' Scott said. 'Is that all? Mrs Loveday made it sound like he was a serial killer or something. Does he have any more recent convictions?'

Jack shook his head sadly. 'Nothing. Shame, really. Sounds like he was quite a guy.' He pointed at a paragraph further down in the article. *'Morley (16) stole the Jaguar XJS belonging to Mr Andrew Bagshott, headmaster of Carrickstowe Secondary School. He drove the vehicle at high speed for several hours before parking it on the Carrickstowe Golf Course.* Nicking the Head's car! Got to admit, the boy had class,' Jack laughed.

Scott glanced up at the clock. The morning was half over and they didn't have much progress to report to Emily yet. But as they left the library and wandered past the newsagent, Scott noticed a display in the window with a big poster saying LOCAL AUTHORS FOR SALE. He spotted several books from the *Heartbreaker History* series by Katherine Trelawney, alias Aunt Kate. There was also a book about bee-keeping, and a pile of slim hardbacks: *Carrickstowe Through the Ages* by G. B. Piggott. Suddenly an idea started to take shape. 'I know!' he said excitedly. 'We'll buy one of

Mr Piggott's books and ask him to sign it for us.'

'Yawn,' Jack groaned, glancing at the book. 'Why would we want to do that? It looks really boring.'

Scott sighed. 'We're not going to *read* it. It's an excuse to go and see Mr Piggott. You know what Dad's like if anyone asks him to sign his book. He's so chuffed he'd probably go round and clean their toilets if they asked him to! Hopefully Piggott's the same and he won't notice if we sneak in a few questions about the disappearing shield.'

'Alright,' Jack conceded as they went in and picked up a copy from the pile. 'But I still can't believe you're going to spend £4.99 on this rubbish.'

Scott patted the cover with its black and white photograph of a Roman coin. 'Don't knock it. This is our ticket into Mr Piggott's office.'

'Yippee!' Jack muttered. He couldn't think of anywhere he'd *less* like to be.

They were turning off the high street on their way to Castle Road, when Scott suddenly grabbed Jack's arm.

'What?' Jack asked. 'You've not clocked another herd of Killer Bulls, have you?'

Scott was staring at the house on the corner. A man was climbing a ladder propped against the front wall.

He'd taken his shirt off and his back – as broad and brown as a table-top – was tattooed with a tapestry of Celtic knots and Chinese dragons.

'Ooh, a man fixing a roof. *How fascinating!*' Jack scoffed.

'Not just *any* man.' Scott pointed at the Transit van parked on the drive. P. MORLEY AND SON, CARPENTERS was painted on the side. *Now* Jack realised what his brother was on about. 'Oh, yeah . . .'

The man on the roof looked down. 'Hey! You two lads!'

Jack jumped and looked round guiltily. Was watching people on ladders a criminal offence in Castle Key?

'Who, us?' Scott called back.

'Don't look so worried,' the man laughed, reversing down the ladder. 'You wouldn't like to earn a bit of pocket money, would you? I need someone to unload the tiles and pass them up to me. My son usually does it, but he's got flu.'

Jack eyed the stacks of tiles in the back of the van. They looked heavy. 'Sorry,' he said. 'We're in a hurry. On our way up to the castle.' Then he winced as Scott's trainer landed a swift kick on the back of his ankle. 'What was *that* for?'

'*Background research,* remember!' Scott hissed. Then he raised his voice. 'Sure! We can help for an hour or so.'

'Cheers, guys.' Pete Morley threw them each a pair of work gloves. 'I wouldn't bother going up to the

66

castle anyway,' he said. 'It's closed after the robbery yesterday. That's why I'm doing this roofing job. I was working on the re-fit for the museum but it's all been put on hold. And if I don't work, I'm losing money.'

Yep! I was right, Jack thought as he picked up the first stack. *These tiles* are *heavy.*

'So, have they found out who stole the Chieftain's Shield from the museum yet?' Scott asked casually, when they took a break for a drink of water. Jack had to admit, Scott was good at the *casual-asking* thing.

Pete Morley kicked a broken tile. 'I wouldn't be surprised if they've pinned it on *me* by now! I was a bit of a bad lad when I was your age, and that Detective Inspector Hassan's got it in for me. But I told him – I was in the museum working on the new display case all morning. I'd have got on faster if Mrs *Busybody* Loveday hadn't kept coming to check up on me and tell me all her gossip, but, even so, I didn't have time to go wandering off nicking things, even if I wanted to. Dovetail joints don't make themselves!'

Scott nodded encouragingly. 'Do you think it was someone who works up at the castle?'

Pete Morley shrugged. 'My money's on one of the security guards. Or Loveday, of course!' He laughed. 'For all we know she's an international jewel thief – when she can spare a few minutes from poking her nose into everyone else's business, that is.'

Jack laughed. But what he really wanted to ask, of course, was how – and *why* – Pete had come up with the *genius* idea of driving the Headmaster's car onto the golf course. He resisted the temptation.

'Back to the grindstone then, lads,' Pete sighed, offering round sticks of MegaMint chewing gum. Then he took another couple of packs from his pocket. 'Have these,' he said. 'They're giving them away as freebies at the newsagent.'

An hour later the boys shifted the last of the tiles and continued their journey up to the castle. The morning sun was beating down and they were both exhausted. Jack shook his arms as he walked. 'My biceps have turned to custard!'

'What biceps?' Scott laughed. 'But at least we've got *something* to report to Emily now. Pete Morley's got an alibi if Mrs Loveday was keeping an eye on him all morning.'

'*And* we earned a tenner each.' Jack waved the note Pete Morley had given him.

'That'll cover the cost of buying Mr Piggott's book,' Scott pointed out. 'This investigating business isn't so hard after all.'

Nine

Breakthrough

Meanwhile Emily and Drift started the morning crouching behind a parked car opposite Lavender Cottage, home of Mrs Irene Loveday, her husband Norman and their collection of golf trophies.

Could Mrs Loveday have stolen the Chieftain's Shield? Emily wondered. She certainly had the Windmill of Opportunity – she was in the castle museum all morning, cleaning, and could easily have slipped away to the storeroom. No doubt she had keys to every room and could have smuggled the shield out in her mop bucket or something. The question was whether she had a motive. Irene Loveday had lived and worked in Castle Key all her life. Why would she suddenly turn to a life of crime?

At 9.30 a.m. the door opened and Mrs Loveday emerged, pulling a little tartan shopping cart. Emily made a note in her book and then followed at a discreet distance, along Magpie Close, across the common and into the high street. Mrs Loveday bought a paper and some cat food at the newsagent. Emily noticed Jack and Scott on their way out. Scott was carrying a book called *Carrickstowe Through the Ages.* They didn't see her, of course. Then Mrs Loveday chatted to Mrs Roberts for ten minutes outside the Post Office. So far, Emily thought, this had the makings of a very tedious morning.

Next, Mrs Loveday called in at the library. Dogs weren't allowed inside so Emily gave Drift the *Keep Watch* command and left him sitting on the step, before tiptoeing after her. Mrs Loveday was already sitting at one of the computers. Emily put on a floppy hat she kept in her bag for just such a purpose and pulled it down over her face. She browsed her way along the shelves. Mrs Loveday was tapping urgently at the keyboard.

What's she doing? Emily wondered. Researching the market price of Saxon shields? Or was she just filling out a tax form?

But when Emily got close enough to glance over her shoulder, she saw that Mrs Loveday was playing On-line poker. And judging by the way she kept tutting and banging her hand down on the mouse, she *wasn't* on a winning streak.

Emily felt the hairs stand up on the back of her neck. This was a breakthrough. *Gambling debts!* The perfect motive! Come to think of it, Mrs Loveday was a regular at the Friday night poker games at Dotty's café too. It was all falling into place: Mrs Loveday had run up huge debts playing poker – probably without her husband knowing anything about it – and now she was in dire need of funds to pay them off; *funds she planned to raise from the theft of the Chieftain's Shield*!

Hardly able to contain her excitement, Emily crept out of the library and retrieved Drift. She loitered in Fish Alley waiting to see what Mrs Loveday would do next. When she came out of the library twenty minutes later and hurried straight across the high street to the bank, Emily was more convinced than ever: *Irene Loveday was up to her eyeballs in debt!*

Emily pulled her phone out of her bag and snapped a photo. She wanted to follow Mrs Loveday inside, but she knew a kid wandering into a bank would attract attention.

Suddenly she had an idea. 'Keep Watch!' she murmured, leaving Drift outside as she took a five-pound note out of her purse and rushed in through the door.

Mrs Loveday was already at the counter. 'I'd like to pay some money into my account. I've just had a little win on the lottery,' she said.

Ha! Emily thought. *Paying money in. She must have sold the shield already.*

The lady behind the counter was glaring over her glasses at Emily. 'Can I help you?' she asked.

Emily waved the five-pound note. 'I just found this on the pavement outside. I wondered if Mrs Loveday had dropped it.'

'Ooh, let me check.' Mrs Loveday fished around in a purse the size of a toaster. 'Oh yes, I *am* short of a five-pound note. Thank you, dear.'

It hadn't crossed Emily's mind that Mrs Loveday might actually claim the money as her own, but now she had no choice but to hand it over.

'It's so refreshing to see honesty in young people,' Mrs Loveday said. She took a twenty-pence piece out of her purse. 'Take this. A little reward.'

'No, thank you,' Emily forced a smile and made for the door.

'Come on, Drift,' she said. 'Honesty in young people? Huh! What about a bit of honesty in *old* people?'

But Emily couldn't stay angry for long. In fact, she was almost skipping by the time she came out on the seafront and headed for Dotty's café. Her Surveillance Operation had been a total success! She had just enough change left for a celebratory banana split, and sat down at one of the tables outside to share it with Drift, while writing up her notes.

It's hardly worth investigating the other suspects, she thought. *Mrs Loveday is definitely our culprit.* She scooped cream onto a wafer and passed it under the table to Drift. He wagged his tail and pricked up his left ear. 'Oh, OK then, I suppose you're right,' she sighed, 'a good detective never jumps to conclusions. I'll track down Victoria White and interview her.' Emily took out her phone, called Directory Enquiries and asked for the number for Roshendra Farm.

It was Victoria's mother, Mrs White, who answered. To Emily's surprise, Victoria was at the museum.

'Mr Piggott asked her to go in today,' Mrs White explained. 'Although I said she should take the day off. Vicky's been so upset by the robbery. The Carrickstowe Hoard was discovered in one of our fields when she was a little girl, you know. We sold our share to the British Museum, but we still feel *attached* to the Hoard – as if it's our responsibility to look after it, in a way. That's why she was so keen to help with the exhibition.' Mrs White paused. 'Sorry, dear, I don't suppose you're interested in all that ancient history. Now, why did you want Vicky? Can I give her a message?'

Oh, I'm very interested, Emily thought. 'I was just wondering whether Vicky would be available again if I can persuade Mum she needs help at The Lighthouse a couple of evenings a week,' she improvised. Mum and

Dad had decided to do without extra help in the kitchen this summer because money was tight – which meant Emily kept getting drafted in instead. It was *slave labour!*

'I'll ask her,' Mrs White said, 'but she's very busy studying in the evenings. She's got a big exam after the holidays. Computer Science is a tough course. I think I'll stick to sheep and cows and rabbits myself!'

As Emily hung up she mulled over Mrs White's words. She vaguely remembered reading about how the Carrickstowe Hoard had been found by some guy with a metal detector on Roshendra Farm land. Now Victoria White had been working at the museum when part of it was stolen! But why would Vicky want to *steal* the shield when her family had already made a fortune from selling it to the British Museum? Mrs White said that Vicky felt *responsible* for the Carrickstowe Hoard. Maybe she wanted the shield, not for the money, but to keep it to herself? It sounded unlikely, but there was only one way to find out. Emily needed to talk to Victoria herself.

'Come on, Drift,' she said.' Back to the castle!'

Ten

An Inside Job

Jack stifled a yawn. He'd spent so long gazing around Mr Piggott's office, it would be etched into his brain for all eternity: computers, old books, antique maps, stone floor, oriental rugs . . . They'd been trapped for over an hour and The Pigster was *still* droning on about the history of Carrickstowe. The worst part was he hadn't got past the Iron Age yet!

Scott had been right, of course. Mr Piggott was ecstatic when they knocked on his door and asked him to sign their copy of his book.

'Ah, excellent!' he enthused. 'Interested in history? Like father, like sons, eh?'

Well, that's where you're wrong, mate, Jack thought. As far as he was concerned, history was the dullest subject ever invented. And archaeology was the dullest of the dull! It wouldn't be so bad if you always found cool stuff like shields and swords, but, most of the time, it was just broken pottery and animal bones. He tried his best to look as if he was totally riveted by first-century cooking pots.

There was a brief respite when Mr Piggott called through to Victoria White in the next-door office and asked her to bring him a cup of tea and some Cokes for the boys. She brought a plate of chocolate biscuits too. She was pretty, Jack noticed, in an outdoorsy kind of way, with flushed cheeks and reddish blonde hair in a ponytail.

Mr Piggott smiled. 'Ah, Victoria! What would I do without you?'

Scott snapped open his Coke and took a biscuit. He'd not been paying much attention to *Iron Age Carrickstowe* either. He'd been trying – and failing – to steer the conversation towards more recent events, like yesterday's robbery. Mr Piggott was clearly not a man who liked to be interrupted. When he finally took a sip of tea, Scott seized his chance.

'What about the Carrickstowe Hoard? That must be one of the most important finds in the area. I was really looking forward to seeing it . . .'

'Ah, yes,' Mr Piggott put down his tea and placed his hands together as if about to pray. He pushed his glasses up with his fingertips and rubbed the bump on the bridge of his nose. Suddenly he rocked forward in his chair.

At last! Scott thought. *He's going to say something about the missing shield.*

'To fully understand the *significance* of the Carrickstowe Hoard,' Mr Piggott began, 'you have to look further back to developments in the late Iron Age . . .'

Jack almost choked on his Coke. This was a nightmare! Like being stuck in an infinite detention with the Teacher from Hell. He leapt up so quickly he knocked his chair clattering to the stone floor. 'Sorry, sorry,' he muttered as he stumbled towards the door, tripping on the edge of a rug. 'Got to go . . . go to the . . . er, toilet. Yes, that's it, *toilet*. Back soon!'

Once through the door, Jack checked his watch. How long could he feasibly take to go to the loo before he had to return to the Office of Doom? Ten minutes? Perhaps if he suddenly developed third-degree constipation he could stretch it to fifteen?

He looked around. He was in a stone passageway,

with dark wood panelling halfway up the walls. To the right he could see the double doors into the modern building that housed the museum and shop. To the left, the corridor led further into the old castle kitchens. He glimpsed a flight of steps leading down to a lower floor. That looked interesting. Maybe there was time for a little exploration . . .

Orange plastic tape had been looped across the stairs. Jack hesitated. It wouldn't hurt just to have a quick peek, would it? *After all,* he thought, stepping over the tape, *the loos might be down here. And if they really wanted to keep people out, they'd have put up a barrier, not just a bit of old ribbon.*

He edged down the stone steps, each one hollowed out by hundreds of years of footsteps. There were niches in the walls where lamps must once have burned, but now the stairwell was lit by the green glow of an emergency light. The walls felt cold under his palms. These stairs must lead to an old cellar or, if he was lucky, maybe even to the *dungeons.*

At the bottom of the stairs there was nothing but a solid metal door fitted with shiny steel padlocks and some kind of electronic security keypad. They really didn't want anyone getting in here! Or getting *out*? Jack pictured a loathsome creature – a troll or an ogre – chained up for thousands of years. Then he snapped back to reality. This door had clearly only been put in recently. He was about to turn around and head back upstairs, but he gave the door a little nudge first. It was bound to be locked, of course . . .

To Jack's amazement, the door swung open on silent hinges.

Just looking for the toilets. Got a bit lost. Jack rehearsed his lines in his head. Then, feeling as though his heart were rocketing around his chest like a ball in a pinball machine, he stepped through the door.

He found himself in a huge room, filled with row upon row of filing cabinets and storage boxes, reaching almost to the ceiling. Wall lamps cast a dim, tawny light and a humming noise came from some kind of air-conditioning contraption. Little red lights blinked on another box high in the corner.

Jack tiptoed along an aisle between banks of cabinets. Labels had been stuck on to the front panels, written in old-style typewriter print on yellowing card: *Flint shards (C. K. Cliff Site, 62a), Medieval fishing floats (Gull Island, 438c), Celtic pins . . . Roman coins . . . Tudor buttons . . .*

He opened a drawer at random and gazed at the tray of tiny arrowheads slowly disappearing from view as he pushed the drawer shut with his thumbs.

He was in the museum storeroom.

Which mean that the safe containing the Carrickstowe Hoard was somewhere in this room! Or rather, the safe containing the Carrickstowe Hoard, minus one shield. *Wouldn't it be cool if I could find a vital clue down here?*

Jack thought. Imagine Scott's face if he, Secret Agent Jack Carter, cracked the case wide open. Even Emily would be impressed!

He'd have to be quick, of course. This was a crime scene! He'd watched enough police dramas on TV to know he was going to be in a whole world of trouble if he was caught wandering around in the middle of it. He'd just find the safe, have a sniff around and then leg it . . .

Achhooo!

Someone sneezed. *And it wasn't Jack!*

What if the burglar had come back? *I could catch them red-handed!* Jack thought. Fizzing with fear and excitement, Jack dropped down and shrank into the shadows. He held his breath and listened. The blood was pumping in his ears like a heavy metal bassline. Maybe he'd imagined the sneeze? He crawled to the end of the row of cabinets, the stone floor biting into his knees with every move. He took a deep breath then peeped out round the last storage box.

He hadn't imagined it.

A figure was bending over a black metal safe the size of a freezer. The figure was huge and kind of ogre-shaped, but it was wearing a grey suit with razor sharp creases down the legs: *Detective Inspector Hassan!*

Jack felt as if the air had gone out of his tyres. He hadn't caught the thief in the act, and he couldn't even get anywhere near the safe to look for that vital clue!

He was just going to have to sneak out before he was caught. *Of course,* he thought crossly, *it all makes sense now. That's why the door's unlocked and the security system is turned off. Those red lights I saw are a motion detector system. If it was operating, an alarm would've started screeching the moment I set foot through the door.*

Suddenly things went from bad to worse. The door banged open. *Someone else had entered the room!* Jack closed his eyes and prayed furiously. *Please don't come down this aisle.* Footsteps rang out, making their way along the aisle between the next two rows of filing cabinets. Jack opened his eyes and breathed again.

'Ah, there you are,' D. I. Hassan boomed. 'Did you call Forensics?'

'Yes. They're sending Tina Johnstone. She'll be here any minute.' The second voice belonged to a woman. It must be another police officer. Jack was about to start inching his way back towards the door – before this Tina person turned up to join the party – when D. I. Hassan spoke again. 'It's obvious even to the naked eye that this safe hasn't been forced.'

'Inside job, you think?' the policewoman asked.

'Must be. No fingerprints of course. Our man – or woman – wore gloves.'

'Someone who had access to the combination then?'

'Looks that way,' Detective Inspector Hassan sighed. '*And* the codes to turn off all the security systems, but

Piggott insists they were all locked up in Fortress Seven . . .' He paused, then sneezed again. Jack peeped out and saw the mighty moustache quivering with the force of the sneeze as if it had a life of its own. D. I. Hassan took a handkerchief from his jacket pocket and blew his nose. 'The dust's setting off my allergies. Come on, let's find the esteemed Mrs Loveday and see if she can rustle us up a cup of tea while we're waiting for Tina.'

Jack didn't wait to hear any more. He scurried along the aisle, slipped through the door and bolted up the stairs. He was almost at the top, *almost safe*!

He looked up. A figure was standing at the top of the stairs, silhouetted against the light from the corridor above.

Tina from Forensics!

Jack felt his stomach turn inside out. The game was up! He was on the wrong side of the orange tape and the police had him surrounded.

Eleven

Investigation Overload

Emily peered down the dingy stairwell. Jack's blue eyes were like frisbees and his face was mushroom-white. Had he seen a ghost? And what was he doing behind the crime-scene tape, anyway?

'Emily!' Jack panted, 'Thank God!'

For one horrible moment, Emily thought he was going to kiss her. She shrank back.

'I thought you were Tina Johnstone,' Jack explained,

looking back over his shoulder.

'Tina *who*?'

'Tell you later. Police . . . after . . . me . . .' Jack panted, racing up the stairs.

Emily stared at Jack in horror. 'What have you done?'

He shook his head. 'Nothing.'

Confused, Emily started back along the corridor. 'Come on, let's get out of here.'

'We've got to rescue Scott first,' Jack whispered.

Emily groaned. What on earth had the boys got up to while she was gone? Had she made the biggest mistake of her career by involving them in this case? 'Tell me the police aren't after *him* too!'

'No. We have to rescue him from being bored senseless by Mr Piggott. He's probably a gibbering wreck by now.' Jack paused for a moment and grinned. 'Although, would we even notice the difference?'

Moments later, Emily was pressing her ear to the door to Mr Piggott's office. Jack did the same. They could hear voices inside. Then the door opened. They both tumbled into the arms of a very surprised Scott.

'What . . . ' Scott spluttered, pushing Jack and Emily ahead of him like a human snow-plough. Then he called back into the room. 'Here's Jack now! Well, we'll be off then. Thank you very much.'

'Where've you *been*?' Scott hissed at Jack.

'Long story,' Jack laughed.

'Well, it'd better be a good one. I had to tell Mr Piggott

you had medical issues to explain how you could take half an hour in the loo.'

Jack elbowed Scott hard. 'Oh, thanks, mate. Thanks very much!'

Emily giggled. She still had no idea what was going on, but at least it seemed neither of the boys had been arrested or blown their cover.

They hurried out of the museum. Drift was waiting patiently on the step on Lookout Duty. He didn't have any significant sightings to report, but sprang around in delight to see Emily, Scott and Jack again. Tail wagging, he led the way to the Tower Room hide-out – which Emily had decided to use as the official HQ for Operation Shield.

'And we can have our lunch there too,' Jack said, patting the small backpack Scott was carrying. 'I hope Aunt Kate's given us loads of sandwiches. All that adrenaline has made me *ravenous*!'

'So, what's new?' Emily said.

They all laughed.

No, Emily thought. *It wasn't a mistake. I'm glad I've got the boys on my team.*

⌒

'OK,' Scott said, 'who wants to go first?' He felt that as the oldest he should start taking the lead a bit more, even though Emily was the most experienced investigator.

'Me, me, ooh pick me!' Jack shouted through a mouthful of cheese and pickle, waving his hand in the air.

'Go on then. What *were* you up to on the Great Toilet Expedition?'

Jack explained how he'd 'accidentally' found himself in the museum storeroom.

Emily stared at him, a ham sandwich halfway to her mouth. 'Wow! There must've been *loads* of brilliant clues down there.'

'Yeah, well, it was a bit crowded with old Hassan around. And then this policewoman showed up.'

'What were they doing? Did they say anything?' Scott asked impatiently.

Jack closed his eyes, re-living the minutes he'd spent crouching behind a cabinet. He'd been more concerned about escaping than finding clues at the time, but he remembered D. I. Hassan saying something about allergies and a cup of tea. And before that . . . they were talking about . . . *Of course!* He *had* found a brilliant clue after all. He jumped up and did a little victory dance. 'Go me! Go me!' he chanted. He hadn't felt this pleased with himself since he'd pulled off that jaw-dropping three-sixty in the Under Thirteen BMX Freestyle Challenge.

'Is there something you want to share with us?' Scott asked. 'In your own time, of course,' he added, rolling his eyes.

Jack stopped dancing and sat down. 'Hassan said it was an inside job, because whoever carried out the robbery must have had the security combinations and codes.' He paused for effect. 'And he said that Mr Piggott keeps all that stuff locked up in a place called . . . er . . .' Jack tugged at his hair, struggling to recall the name. 'Fortress something. Fortress Seven, that's it!'

Emily pulled out her notebook and started scribbling furiously. 'Right. We've got to find out where this fortress is . . . '

Scott laughed.

'What's so funny?' Emily asked.

'Fortress Seven isn't a *place*. It's a computer program for keeping secret information safe. It's meant to be really hard to break into.'

'Well that rules out Mrs Loveday,' Jack said. 'I can't see her as a hacker. She probably doesn't even know how to use a computer.'

Emily laughed and shook her head. 'Oh, yes, she does! She was on the computer in the library this morning playing on-line poker. In fact, I'm pretty sure she's the thief!' She snapped her notebook shut, enjoying the flabbergasted looks on the boys' faces. 'Irene Loveday has a gambling problem,' she announced dramatically. 'She plays poker on-line *and* at Dotty's on Friday nights too. She's run up massive debts. I have photographic evidence of her going to the bank to pay in money this morning.'

'Er, paying money into a bank isn't exactly a crime,' Scott pointed out.

'It is if you're paying in the proceeds from selling stolen property,' Emily retorted. 'And there's more. Mrs Loveday *claims* she was polishing doorknobs in the corridor all morning, but they *weren't even that shiny*. I was checking them when I ran into Jack escaping from the storeroom.'

Jack shrugged. 'That's probably because she kept skiving off to see how Pete Morley was getting on with the display cabinet.'

Emily wasn't going to give up on her theory that easily. 'Well, Mrs Loveday is still *my* Number One Suspect.'

'Talking of Pete Morley,' Scott said, 'I don't think he did it. He was slaving away on that roof this morning. Why would he bother if he'd just nicked something so valuable?'

'I agree with Scott – for once,' Jack said. 'Pete Morley's cool.'

'And what about Geoff Piggott?' Emily asked.

Jack rolled on the ground clutching his head as if in agony. 'Don't remind me!'

Scott grinned. 'I didn't get much out of him. Well, not much *relevant*, I mean. According to Mrs Loveday, he was in his office on the phone all morning. And why would he *want* to steal the shield anyway? Having the Carrickstowe Hoard at the museum is his dream come true.'

'Hmm,' Emily mused, writing in her book, *Geoff Piggott. No apparent motive.* Then she flicked through the notes from her interview with Victoria White. 'I spoke to Vicky just now. She says she was in her office doing paperwork all yesterday morning, except when taking cups of tea round for the others.'

'But she could easily have popped down to the storeroom?' Scott said.

'I suppose so,' Emily agreed reluctantly. She'd pretty much ruled Vicky out of her enquiries. She was so friendly and hard-working and clever. *Clever?* Suddenly Emily remembered something Mrs White mentioned on the phone.

'What is it?' Scott asked.

'Oh, just that Vicky's doing a degree in Computer Science,' Emily mumbled.

'And?' Jack made a *so-what* face. 'That's not illegal, is it?'

But Scott had made the connection just as quickly as Emily had. 'Victoria might know how to hack into the Fortress Seven software and get the security codes!'

Emily nodded slowly. She didn't like to admit it, but it was true. *And* Vicky's office was next-door to Mr Piggott's. She'd have loads of chances to sneak in and get onto his computer.

'So, basically, it's a toss-up between Mrs Loveday and Victoria White,' Jack said, palming the last piece of cherry cake.

'Well, we haven't even *started* on the security guards yet,' Emily pointed out.

'Aggh! My brain hurts,' Jack laughed. 'I've got Investigation Overload. Can Not Compute,' he said in a robot voice. 'Must Reboot System.'

Emily laughed. 'Me too.' She jumped to her feet. 'Come on, let's go to the beach.'

Twelve

An Unexpected Encounter

Drift ran around in circles chasing his tail. *Beach* was one of his favourite words.

'Let's take *Gemini* and row round the other side of the bay to Pirate Cove,' Emily said, as they set off down Castle Road.

'Pirate Cove? Count me in,' Jack said eagerly.

Emily grinned. 'It's a lovely sandy beach, and it's just past the . . .'

'. . . the Whistling Caves?' Scott completed her sentence. 'You want to go and see if they've started up again, don't you?'

Emily grinned. 'Yeah. I haven't had a chance to talk to Old Bob about the caves yet. He's gone off on a deep-sea fishing trip for a few days.'

'Shall I bring my ear-plugs?' Jack teased, as he climbed over the stile into the cow field.

Emily gave him a shove. Jack toppled backwards and landed with a splat in a very large, very wet cowpat. The cows looked on with mild interest. Scott and Emily, on the other hand, were laughing so much they could hardly walk.

'Nice one, Em,' Scott gasped. 'Couldn't have done better myself!'

'Uggh!' Jack groaned. 'Green poo! I'll have to go home and get changed.'

'Too right,' Scott said, holding his nose. 'You stink!'

'Meet me at *Gemini* in an hour,' Emily said, and, with that, she – and Drift, of course – took off across the meadow.

~

They took turns to row and were soon rounding Lighthouse Point and approaching the cliffs. Jack looked across at the caves. Unlike on their last visit, there was no strip of shingle at the foot of the caves.

In fact, the waves were rolling right inside the lower caverns.

'It's high tide this afternoon,' Emily explained. 'When we came in the morning last time, the tide was out.'

Suddenly Drift's ears pricked up and quivered like antennae. Moments later, Jack could hear it too. Even above the constant wailing of the gulls, there was no mistaking the piercing whistling sound. Emily grinned. *Told you so* was written so clearly across her face it was practically in neon lights.

Jack shook his head and frowned. 'Nope, still can't hear anything.'

Scott and Emily gaped at him.

'Are you deaf or something?' Scott asked.

'Only kidding,' Jack laughed, putting his hands over his ears. 'Is there a volume control on those caves?'

They rowed on, round another headland to a hidden cove. Pirate Cove was a perfect half-moon of white sand, sheltered on each side by jumbles of giant rocks. They pulled *Gemini* onto the sand, then Scott and Emily swam while Jack and Drift ran around on the beach chasing tiny crabs. Later, they gathered driftwood and built a campfire. Aunt Kate had come up with the awesome suggestion that they cook their supper on the beach, and she'd packed a cold-box with everything they'd need. Jack gazed into the flames and listened to the sausages sizzling in the pan. Scott was poking at the embers with a stick. Jack caught his eye, and they both grinned.

'Smashing!' Jack sighed.

'Smashing!' Scott agreed. Then he looked up. 'Hey, what are you doing with those sausages – cooking them or cremating them?'

Emily lounged on a sun-baked rock, watching the boys cook. She'd had to show them how to set a fire properly, but they seemed to be managing on their own now. She wriggled her toes in the cool sand. Curled up at her side, Drift twitched in his sleep. Emily sighed happily. It had been a fabulous day. She had a Really Significant Investigation to get her teeth into, two great new friends *and* the caves were whistling again. What could be better?

'Sausages are ready!' Jack shouted.

—

Next morning Emily was in the kitchen munching on a piece of toast when she had a brainwave. She ran back up the stairs – all one hundred and twenty of them – to her room, grabbed her phone and called Scott's number.

'Maybe it's a morning thing,' she said.

'Er, am I supposed to have any idea what you're talking about?' Scott asked.

'Oh, sorry,' Emily giggled. 'The caves! I've been

thinking about it all night, trying to figure out why they weren't whistling on Monday. What if they've only stopped whistling in the *mornings*?'

'They like a lie-in, you mean?' Scott said. 'I know how that feels!'

Emily ignored him. 'We were there at 10.30 a.m. on Monday, weren't we? I'm going to go back there at exactly the same time this morning and check it out. You guys coming?'

'On our way!'

Jack took the oars. He was getting quite good at rowing now, though he said so himself. He was going to look like Arnold Schwarzenegger by the end of the summer. But he didn't really get what all the fuss was about the whistling. They were caves! Who knew how they operated? Sometimes they whistled, sometimes they didn't. So what? But Emily seemed to think it was important – so important, in fact, that she'd put off their plan to pursue enquiries with the two security guards until the afternoon. *Pursue enquiries?* Jack thought. *I'm starting to sound like Emily now.*

'To whistle or not to whistle?' Scott recited, in a theatrical Shakespearean Actor voice. 'That is the question!'

They didn't have to wait long for the answer.

The caves weren't whistling.

Nor were they trilling or warbling or fluting or piping.

They were just sitting there, being caves. In silence.

'Looks like you were right, Em,' Scott said. 'These caves just don't *do* mornings!'

'I bet Old Bob's got a saying about this,' Jack laughed. '*No whistling in the morn . . . your pants will get torn!*'

'*. . . watch out for frogspawn!*' Scott suggested.

Emily started to say something but suddenly Drift jumped up onto the bow of the boat and started barking. 'He's seen something!' she shouted.

Jack peered across the waves towards the cliffs. 'A seagull? A cloud? Give us a clue, Drift. What's the first letter?'

'Look! There's someone there,' Scott said. 'At the Whistling Caves.'

Jack pulled on the oars until they were close enough to make out the figure on the tiny pebbly beach exposed by the low tide: mad-professor hair, glasses, tweedy trousers . . .

'What's *Mr Piggott* doing here?' Scott asked.

'Dunno!' Jack said. 'But let's not stop to find out in case he starts going on about the Iron Age again!'

Emily frowned. 'He might be stranded. I can't see his boat.' She cupped her hands around her mouth.

'Hey, Mr Piggott! Are you OK?'

Mr Piggott – who had been about to disappear into the dark hollow of the largest cave – whipped round so fast his glasses flew off. He knelt down and began fumbling around on the shingle.

When he finally found them, he took some time wiping the lenses and placing them back on his nose. His face was red and he didn't look terribly pleased to be disturbed. 'Oh, it's you three!' he said, squinting out at the boat. He managed to force a smile. 'Super afternoon, eh, kids?' Mr Piggott spoke in a chirpy tone that Jack knew well; it was the one teachers always used when they were trying to convince you that a surprise test was going to be fun. 'I thought I'd just row out for a relaxing spin around the bay. Very stressful time at the museum with the Chieftain's Shield being stolen, you know.'

Scott waved. 'OK, we'll leave you in peace, then.'

Jack was already rowing. 'We're out of here,' he muttered, 'before he sucks us into his Web of Boredom!'

Emily leapt up so suddenly she almost capsized the boat. 'Of course! Mr Piggott is the thief! He's obviously got the shield with him and is about to row off with it . . .'

'I didn't *see* a getaway boat,' Scott said.

'It must have been tied up behind one of the rocks,' Emily replied. 'He couldn't have got to the caves any other way. I bet he's rowing out to meet an accomplice who's waiting for him on a larger vessel. Almost certainly a millionaire with a yacht. Yes, he'll be the one who's going to *buy* the shield.'

'I thought you said the thief was *definitely* Mrs Loveday?' Jack had to admire Emily's imagination, but sometimes it was hard to keep up.

'Well, new evidence has come to light now!' Emily retorted.

'You're right,' Scott said. 'It's dead suspicious.'

'I'm calling D. I. Hassan.' Emily took her phone from the waterproof bag tucked under the seat of the boat. 'Oh, no. No reception. We're too close to the cliffs.'

'I haven't got a signal either,' Scott said, checking his phone. 'We'll have to row like crazy and hope we can get back to The Lighthouse before he gets too far away. I'll take the oars for a bit.'

As they approached the inlet, Emily jumped out and waded for shore. She spotted someone climbing the steps to The Lighthouse. 'Dad!' she yelled. 'Quick! Can you help Scott and Jack moor up? I've got a vital phone call to make!'

'Whoah, slow down there, kiddo,' Dad laughed, as he turned and started back down the steps. 'You guys have missed all the excitement. It's all over the village!'

'What's happened?' Emily was already halfway up the path – but she couldn't resist hanging back to find out what the 'excitement' was. Although, knowing Dad, it was probably just a new variety of organic turnips at the greengrocer's.

'There's been another theft at the Castle museum,' Dad said. 'The Ceremonial Helmet and the King's Sword have been taken this time.'

Thirteen

Seriously Strange

'Well, we can cross *one* of our prime suspects off the list,' Scott said. He was sitting with Emily and Jack on the harbour wall, trying to make sense of the new turn of events. From what Emily's Dad said, the theft had taken place about three quarters of an hour ago. But they had seen Mr Piggott at the Whistling Caves just over *half* an hour ago. That would've given him less than fifteen minutes, after stealing the helmet and the sword, to get down to the harbour and row round to the caves.

'He can't have done it, even if he was an Olympic rower,' Scott went on. 'It took us half an hour to row back from the caves on full-sprint-mode. And my arms are feeling every minute of it.'

'I know,' Emily sighed. 'There goes *my* theory! He couldn't even have got there in a *speedboat* in that time. And even a professional climber would have taken hours to get over the promontory and climb along the cliff-face to the caves.'

'Time travel?' Jack suggested. 'Maybe that's how he knows so much about the Iron Age!'

Scott laughed. It was so confusing. They'd all been convinced that Mr Piggott's shifty behaviour at the Whistling Caves proved that he was the thief.

'He has the perfect alibi this time,' Emily said. 'The four of us!'

'Four?' Jack echoed.

'Yeah, Drift saw him first, remember?'

Recognising his name, Drift sat up. His black ear was flopped across his eye and the white one with brown spots was standing up straight. *I know that ear formation*, Jack thought. *Drift's hungry!* 'Me too, mate,' he said. 'Let's go to the café and get fish and chips.'

Sitting outside Dotty's Tea Rooms eating their lunch, the friends continued to puzzle over their investigation.

Emily took out her notebook, brushed off a cluster of little black thunderbugs and drew a line through Mr Piggott's name.

Jack gave the bottom of the ketchup bottle two swift thumps. Suddenly an idea popped into his head. 'There *might* be two separate thieves!' he pointed out. 'What if The Pigster nicked the shield and then someone *else* took the helmet and sword?'

Emily chewed her pen. 'Yeah, that's a good point, Jack.'

Jack grinned. Emily and Scott were clearly gobsmacked that he'd come up with such a brilliant idea. He was pretty amazed himself, come to think of it. He brandished a chunk of battered cod on his fork. 'They say fish is Brain Food. Here, you try some, Drifty. You could be on *Dog Mastermind* with this.'

Emily laughed. But then she got that business-like look in her dark eyes again. 'We'll have to go up to the museum,' she said. 'We need to find out whether any of the other suspects have alibis for this morning. And,' she added, 'we'll have to re-name Operation Shield, of course, now that other stuff is missing too. I vote we call it Operation Treasure.'

They were turning into Castle Road when D. I. Hassan's police car sped down the hill and turned right, heading towards Carrickstowe. Emily couldn't be sure, but she thought she glimpsed a figure sitting in the back seat. Had someone been arrested before she'd even had a chance to complete her investigation?

They raced up the hill. When they reached the top no one was around. Emily signalled for them all to establish an observation post behind Victoria White's Mini, which was parked close to the museum entrance.

Moments later, Mrs Loveday emerged and stood in the doorway, dabbing her nose with a handkerchief. 'Oh, good heavens!' she was exclaiming to someone behind her, 'An *arrest*! What a turn-up for the books! A common thief in our midst all this time!'

The person behind Mrs Loveday handed her a mug. *Probably Victoria White*, Emily thought. *Vicky's usually on tea-making duty at the museum.*

Mrs Loveday sank down on a bench looking out over the car park, fanning her face with her handkerchief. The tea-maker stepped forward out of the shadows.

It was a man with tattoos scrolling down his arms from under his t-shirt.

Emily gasped.

'Pete Morley,' Jack breathed.

That meant the person being taken off in the police car was . . .

'Victoria White!' Mrs Loveday wailed. 'Well, of course, I always had my suspicions.'

Victoria White. Kind, friendly Vicky had stolen the

Saxon treasure. Emily could hardly believe it. Nor, it seemed, could Pete Morley.

'Nah! Can't see it myself,' he said, leaning against the door-frame, chewing gum and cradling his tea mug in his hands. 'Her family made a fortune when the Hoard was found on their land. They sold it to the British Museum, didn't they? Vicky doesn't need the dosh.'

Mrs Loveday looked disapprovingly at her tea. 'Well, with some people, the more they have the more they want. Victoria White's obviously been spoilt rotten by all that wealth.'

'Ooh, that's so *unfair*!' Emily hissed. 'Vicky's not *like* that. She's always worked to earn her own money.'

But Mrs Loveday clearly had different views. 'Oh, no, it's just take, take, take for Little Miss White! Looking After Number One. Never mind innocent people like me having a Clown of Suspicion hanging over them. And that Inspector Hasseem had the cheek to ask for the key to my cleaning cupboard yesterday! He rummaged through all my chemicals. Made a terrible mess of them.'

Pete Morley shrugged. 'Think what you like. But I'm sure they've got the wrong person.'

'You heard what the police said as well as I did,' Mrs Loveday replied. 'They found all the security codes on her laptop. That's Intoxicating Evidence, that is.'

'*Incriminating* evidence, you mean?' Pete Morley corrected, turning to go back inside.

'Precisely,' Mrs Loveday said. '*Highly* Incriminating Evidence.'

'We were right. Victoria must have hacked into Fortress Seven and stolen the codes,' Scott whispered.

Emily nodded sadly. 'Let's go and see what else we can find out.' She turned to Drift and gave him the *Runaway* command, pointing in Mrs Loveday's direction. Drift darted out into the car park and started dashing around at random.

'Pretend we're trying to catch him,' Emily whispered. Then she ran after the little dog, yelling, 'Drift, Drift, you naughty boy! Come here.' By this time, Drift was 'hiding' under the bench, wagging his tail.

'Oh, there you are!' Emily shouted, jogging up to the bench and panting loudly as if she'd just run a marathon. The boys weren't far behind her. 'Oh, sorry, Mrs Loveday. Drift suddenly ran off. He must have seen a rabbit up here.'

'That's alright, dear. I'm just having a little sit down for my nerves.' Mrs Loveday lowered her voice. 'I'm not one to make a Mountain out of a Moleskin, but we've had another robbery! The police have made an *arrest*!' She sat back, waiting for the information to sink in. '*Victoria White.*'

Scott pretended to be taken aback and then switched on the charm. 'How terrible for you! What a shock! Poor Mr Piggott,' he added, fishing for information. 'This *will* be a bombshell for him when he gets back.'

Mrs Loveday smiled adoringly at Scott and patted the bench for him to sit next to her. 'Gets back, dear? Oh, no, Mr Piggott's been here all morning. The poor man's been in his office on the phone, cancelling the arrangements for the Grand Opening of the Exhibition. I could hear him from the corridor.'

'Polishing doorknobs again?' Jack asked innocently.

Mrs Loveday narrowed her eyes suspiciously. '*Dusting* if you must know. The cobwebs in those stone passages will be the death of me!'

But Scott was only half listening. *Mr Piggott's been here all morning?* he thought. *But that's impossible! He was at the Whistling Caves just an hour ago.* Emily was obviously thinking the same thing; she was staring at Mrs Loveday, and – for the first time Scott could remember – she was lost for words.

Scott managed to mask his surprise and made a sympathetic noise – as if he'd been plagued by cobwebs in corridors for years and knew *exactly* how Mrs Loveday felt.

'What was stolen this time?' Emily had regained the power of speech at last.

'The Ceremonial Helmet and the King's Sword. They were missing when the security guards checked the safe. So, of course, Mr Piggott had to call in the police again. They searched all the offices. That's when they discovered Victoria White's Underfoot Activities . . .'

'Under*hand*, you mean?' Jack corrected.

'That's what I said!' Mrs Loveday sniffed, 'And after Mr Piggott went out of his way to give her a job. The ungrateful little minx! Now, I can't sit around here all day, even if you can.'

After Mrs Loveday had bustled off into the museum, no one spoke for several seconds.

It was Emily who broke the silence. 'Mr Piggott was in two places at once?'

'How does *that* work?' Jack asked.

Scott shook his head. He couldn't figure it out either. 'There's something seriously strange going on here!'

Fourteen

Front Page News

The following morning, Scott and Jack were tucking into scrambled eggs and bacon when Aunt Kate came into the kitchen waving a copy of *The Carrickstowe Times*. 'Castle Key's made the front page this morning.'

She dropped the paper on to the table. BLACK DAY FOR WHITE: SAXON THIEF ARRESTED, the headline screamed, above a close-up of Victoria White wearing a sparkly dress, laughing and holding up a glass of wine in a toast. The photo looked as though it had been taken at a party. It made her look like a drunken rich kid.

'Apparently, there've been some thefts up at the museum,' Aunt Kate said, stooping to unload the washing machine.

Scott nodded. 'Oh, yes, we heard about that.'

Jack concentrated on buttering his toast and tried not to laugh. They hadn't *lied* to Aunt Kate about their investigations, but they hadn't exactly told her all about them either. Each evening she asked if they'd had a good day and they gave her a few edited highlights: been rowing, been to the beach . . . that kind of thing. Aunt Kate never asked for details, which was fine by Jack who felt that sharing information with adults should always be on a strictly need-to-know basis. He was dying to read the article, but he didn't want to look *too* interested while Aunt Kate was there. As soon as she went outside to put the washing on the line, he made a grab for the paper.

'Hey, give that back!' Scott protested, snatching it out of his hands.

'I had it first!'

There was a tussle and then a ripping sound: Mr Piggott had been torn in half.

'So *that's* how he can be in two places at once!' Scott laughed.

'Victoria White (19) was arrested yesterday . . .' Jack

read, finally getting hold of the paper '. . . charged with the theft of three Saxon artefacts from Castle Key Museum. The Chieftain's Shield, Ceremonial Helmet and King's Sword were on loan from the British Museum . . .'

It was only when they came to the very last paragraph that the boys found something they hadn't already heard from Mrs Loveday. '. . . White claims to have been in Carrickstowe at the time of the second theft, driving to an appointment at *Gift-Tastic*, supplier of gifts to the museum shop,' Jack read. 'However, both her boss, Geoff Piggott (55) and *Gift-Tastic* Manager, Shane Webb (36) told our reporter, Belinda Baxter, that they had no knowledge of any such appointment . . .'

Aunt Kate came back into the kitchen wiping her glasses on a corner of her apron. 'Phew, it's hot out there. Feels like there's a thunderstorm coming.' The boys hurriedly turned the page and pretended to be reading the cartoons. But it seemed Aunt Kate was as intrigued by the headline story as they were.

'I for one don't believe it was Victoria White,' she said.

'Why not?' Jack asked.

'Well, I don't know anything about computers, but if that girl was smart enough to hack into some fancy data-encryption software, she's not the kind of *dimwit* who'd leave the codes lying around on her laptop where anyone could find them, is she?' Aunt Kate started clearing the breakfast table. 'Sounds like a set-up job to me! Have you finished with that bacon, Jack?'

Jack stared at Aunt Kate in astonishment. *Encrytption software*? For an old lady who lived in the middle of nowhere and knew nothing about computers, she seemed pretty clued up! And where did she get a phrase like *set-up job*? It must be from reading all those spy thrillers on the bookshelf in the living room!

Aunt Kate smiled and wiped her hands on her apron. 'Now, boys, I've got a little job for you. I'm on the rota to clean the church brasses this morning but I've got to write my speech for the Romantic Writers' Conference. Would you pop in and do the brasses for me?'

Scott rubbed polish onto the beak of an eagle that was perched on the pulpit balancing a bible on its outstretched wings. He'd never *seen* so much brass! Candlesticks, railings, plaques, plates . . . they could be here for *weeks*!

'I feel like Mrs Loveday, with her never-ending doorknobs,' Jack complained, flicking his cloth at a brass vase.

Scott laughed. He'd never in a gazillion years admit to anything so spectacularly uncool, but he was secretly quite enjoying himself. The church was peaceful, the sun shining in through the stained-glass windows was splashing rainbow colours across the floor, and while he worked he could think things over. Aunt Kate had a point. Why *hadn't* Vicky tried to cover her tracks? If she'd stolen all those codes, she'd have to be a total fruit-loop to leave them on her laptop in her office. He moved on to the eagle's talons. It was weirdly satisfying watching gleaming gold emerge from dull grey. And if Vicky *had* stolen the helmet and the sword yesterday morning, surely she could've faked a more convincing alibi; saying she'd gone to a mythical appointment no one had ever heard of was just *pathetic*!

Scott was so deep in thought that when a wave of sound suddenly cascaded through the church he jumped and banged his head on the bible. The can of polish dropped from his hand and rolled towards the altar.

Duh-duh-duh-duuuuuuuuuh! The momentous sound was swelling louder and louder. It was like being caught inside the soundtrack of a horror movie.

Scott looked around. Then he laughed. He couldn't believe he hadn't noticed it before. The organ filled almost the entire back wall. Surrounded by an ornately carved wooden frame, the metal pipes soared to the rafters.

'Tell me we don't have to polish *those*!' Jack laughed.

They couldn't see who was playing the organ until they found their way to a small flight of stairs that led up behind the pipes. At the top a man was sitting hunched over a bank of keyboards, hands and feet jerking in every direction like some kind of body-popping string puppet, as he worked the pedals and stops that stuck out at every angle.

Suddenly the music subsided and the organist turned round. He was wearing a black shirt and white vicar's collar, but the rest of his appearance was less traditional: a full set of biker's leathers, a tuft of purple hair in the middle of an otherwise shaved head, and a row of silver rings through one eyebrow. Jack tried not to stare. The man's outfit would look pretty tame in London, but in Castle Key church it was like spotting a flamingo in a duck pond.

'Ah, hello boys. Nice to see you helping out! I'm Colin Warnock, the curate here at St. Michael's.' He held out his hand, then looked down at it and grinned. Two of his fingers were strapped together in a bandage. 'Makes playing the Wedding March a bit of a challenge,' he chuckled, 'But hey ho, God works in mysterious ways.'

'What happened?' Scott asked.

'Ooh, was it the organ?' Jack asked. He had no idea what the inner workings of a church organ were like but they sounded like they could easily mangle fingers in disgustingly gory ways.

Colin Warnock smiled. 'Oh, no, something much less Godly, I'm afraid. Came off my motorbike taking the corner a bit too fast out near Westward Beach.' He turned back to the keyboard and started to play.

114

Magnificent chords resounded all around the church. The tune was familiar but it wasn't a hymn. Suddenly Scott realized Colin was playing *Bohemian Rhapsody* by Queen! He wished he had his guitar with him to join in. Jack started to sing along, using his can of polish as a microphone. They both applauded as Colin built to a crescendo and held the last note. 'Way cool!' Jack said.

'You want a go?' Colin asked.

Jack grinned as he sat down and attacked the keyboard in his mad-pianist impression. Scott clapped his hands over his ears. It sounded like a set of bagpipes being run over by a bus!

'That's Cruelty To Ears, that is,' Colin laughed. 'Let me show you.' He sat down next to Jack. 'These stops open and close the pipes. When you change the length of the pipes, you change the sound . . .'

Scott wandered back to the pulpit to finish polishing his eagle, half-listening to Jack's organ tutorial. He winced as Jack produced a flat honk followed by a toe-curling screech. But something Colin had said was tugging away at a little thread in his brain. It was like waking up in the morning, trying to remember a dream. It kept slipping away. But then suddenly he caught hold of it. 'Yes!' he cried, punching the air.

He'd just had the biggest brainwave since microwave popcorn!

Fifteen

Brainwaves All Round

S cott closed his eyes and let the full impact of his
brainwave sink in. *If organ pipes can change their
sound depending on whether they're open or closed,
other things can too!* he thought.

He pulled his phone out of his pocket and texted
Emily*: Meet @ Gemini ASAP!*

'Come on,' he shouted to Jack over the organ recital.
'We've got to go!'

'But I want to stay,' Jack objected. 'This organ is awesome.'

'You can come back another day,' Colin laughed. 'I've got to sort my hymns out now anyway. I'll teach you to play the *Star Wars* theme next time.'

After the cool of the church, the sweltering heat outside felt like stepping into a sauna. 'What's going on?' Jack asked, jogging to catch up with Scott as he raced across the graveyard and into Church Lane.

'I'll tell you when we meet Emily.'

—

Emily was in The Lighthouse kitchen, helping Mum chop tomatoes for the lunchtime buffet, when Scott's text popped up on her phone. She dropped her knife into the sink. 'Sorry, Mum. Got to go. Something's come up.'

'That wouldn't be your new boyfriend by any chance, would it?' Mum asked.

'It was *Scott*, if that's who you mean.'

Mum winked. 'Ah, yes, the older one. Tall, green eyes, floppy sun-streaked hair. *Very* dishy!'

'M-u-u-u-m,' Emily protested. 'Scott's so *not* my boyfriend. And if you ever say *dishy* again I'll run away from home!'

'Have a nice date,' Mum teased, as Emily flew

off down the spiral stairs – followed by Drift, of course.

—

'So, what's up?' Emily demanded, as the boys ran towards her. She'd arrived at the inlet first and had already untied *Gemini* from the mooring ring.

Jack shrugged. 'Search me!' he panted. 'One minute we're polishing brass eagles and playing the organ. The next minute Scott's gone all *mys-ter-i-o-s-o*. Must've had a Religious Experience or something.'

Emily shook her head. 'Maybe if I just *wait* long enough this will start making sense.'

Scott pushed *Gemini* out into the waves and hopped in. 'I'll explain on the way to the Whistling Caves.' He took the oars and began to row.

'Still waiting for that explanation . . . ' Emily said, as soon as they were heading out towards the end of Lighthouse Point.

'It was in the church,' Scott said, 'when I heard Colin explaining how you use the stops to open and close the organ pipes and make them play different sounds . . .' He stopped rowing for a moment and looked at the others as if expecting them to suddenly see the light. Drift was the only one who didn't have a blank look on his face.

'Er, where are you going with this?' Jack asked.

Scott sighed. 'That's what could be happening with the Whistling Caves!'

'So you're saying there's some kind of giant Colin the Curate pulling stops out of the cliffs?' Jack snorted. 'Sorry, mate, those polish fumes have *definitely* gone to your head!'

Scott ignored him. 'The whistling sound must be caused by the wind travelling through all the holes and passageways in the cliff face, right? So, if the air passage is diverted by opening or closing some kind of trapdoor in one of the caves, it might change the sound – or even stop the whistling altogether.'

Emily stared at Scott, enthralled. But it wasn't Scott's green eyes or floppy hair she was looking at; she was seeing visions of smugglers lashing their boat to the rocks by the light of the moon on a wild, stormy night, unloading barrels of brandy, and signalling with their lanterns to their accomplices high above on the cliff-top to heave open the trapdoor. 'You mean a *secret passage*!'

Scott nodded. 'Exactly. Inside the cliff, leading down from the castle to the sea.'

'Cool!' Jack exclaimed. '*Now* I get it!' Then he had a brainwave of his own. 'Maybe the secret passage was an escape route for the inhabitants of the castle.' He stood up in the middle of the boat. 'In the unlikely event of an attack,' he recited in the style of an air steward, 'your emergency exits are here, here and here. Please remove high-heeled shoes before entering the secret passage.'

Drift bounced around joining in the fun. 'Calm down, Drift,' Emily laughed. 'You'll capsize the boat.' But then it was her turn to jump up. 'Jack, you're a genius!' she cried. 'That's where Old Bob's saying comes from! *If the whistling do cease, the castle shall know no peace.* The caves only stop whistling when someone opens the secret passage to escape; and that means the castle is under siege.'

Jack grinned. No one had ever called him a *genius* before! And he couldn't wait to reach the caves and start searching for the secret passage. As they rounded Lighthouse Point, he strained his ears for the sound of whistling. Drift's ears were trembling. Yes, there it was, the high clear notes piping across the water.

'The trapdoor must be closed at the moment.' Jack looked at Scott and Emily. They were listening to the caves too, their eyes shining with excitement.

If we could find the secret passage, Jack thought, *what an awesome adventure that would be!*

Sixteen

Drift Makes a Discovery

As they drew close to the cliff, Emily slid over the side of the boat and half-waded, half-swam ashore with the mooring rope, her knees scraping on the rocks beneath the surface. It was late morning and she noted that the tide, although still low, had turned and was starting to come back in. Already the waves were creeping up the narrow margin of shingle. She found her footing and hauled *Gemini* in while the boys used the oars to keep the boat from buffeting against the rocks. 'We can't stay here long,' Emily said, as she lassoed the rope around a rock and pulled the bowline knot tight. 'We don't want to get trapped in the caves. The entrance is almost under water at high tide.'

Scott eyed the waves. 'We could come back earlier tomorrow if you don't think it's safe.'

'Don't be such a wimp!' Jack scoffed, already disappearing into the biggest cave. 'Of course,' he called back, 'if you'd rather go home and do some embroidery, feel free, but I'm going to find the secret passage.'

Emily checked her watch. 'It's OK. We'll be fine for another hour or two.'

Jack had to duck to enter the cave, but, once inside, the roof was much higher. The roar of the sea and the keening of the gulls were muted. Even the whistling sound was softer. Jack scrambled over the loose rocks on the cave floor, but then he stumbled and faltered. He couldn't see where he was going. He looked back. Emily and Scott were silhouetted against the window of sunlight in the cave-mouth. 'Scott!' he called.

Scott, Scott, Scott . . . The echo bounced round the cave.

Jack took another step and cursed as a ridge of rock caught him on the forehead. And now he could hear strange noises in the black depths of the cave – a snuffling, panting noise . . .

. . . something soft and furry brushed against his leg.

Jack let out a yell.

'Drift!' Emily called. 'Where are you?'

'Gnnnh!' Jack made a sound halfway between a squeak of terror and a hysterical laugh. 'He's here. Trying to give me a heart attack!'

'There are torches in the boat,' Emily called. 'In the emergency bag with the flare and stuff.'

'Now she tells us!' Jack muttered.

'This time,' Scott said, directing his torch beam in Jack's direction a few moments later, 'let's stick together and work our way round the cave instead of just barging about randomly.'

Even with the torches, searching the cave was a slow process. Scott inched forward, feeling along the wall for holes or gaps. It could take years to find the passage – and this was just *one* of the caves. Just when he was thinking of giving up he felt something. His hand slid across a gap in the wall before coming up against a second bank of rock. 'Quick, shine all the torches here!' he shouted.

The fault-line ran from floor to ceiling. Scott pushed his shoulder into the breach. Sandwiched between the rock faces he shuffled sideways for a few steps until he came out into an open space. He shone the torch around. 'Wow!' he breathed. 'Come and look at this.'

He was standing in a vast chamber. Pillars of rock supported a roof laced with hollows and cavities like a giant sponge. Scott could feel the air vibrating; it sounded almost like the singing of an immense choir.

'Awesome!' Jack said as he emerged from the gap.

Emily followed and shone her torch around the cavern. It was the most magical place she'd ever seen, a hidden world deep inside the cliff. They had entered the very heart of the Whistling Caves.

'What's that?' Jack whispered, shining his torch beam high up on the far wall.

'I can see it. There's something glinting.' Emily was already picking her way across the boulder-strewn cave. She reached up and felt a crevice in the rock. Her fingers touched coarse fabric and then knocked against a hard, metallic edge.

'What is it, Em?' Jack cried. 'Is it the secret passage?'

Unable to speak for excitement, Emily eased the corner of the fabric towards her until the bundle teetered on the brink of the ledge and then fell into her arms. She staggered under the weight. But Scott took the bundle from her and placed it carefully on the ground, where Drift sniffed at it with interest.

Jack pulled the sacking away.

A gold disc, as big as a bicycle wheel, gleamed in the flickering yellow torchlight. Emily gazed in wonder at the dragons, wolves and boars carved into its surface, bordered by a pattern of knots and runes.

'The Chieftain's Shield!' Scott murmured.

'And the Ceremonial Helmet.' Jack hoisted it like a trophy. The brow and nose plate were encrusted with red and amber jewels, burning like coloured fire in the torchlight, as bright as the stained glass in the church. A triple shadow of the helmet was projected on the cave wall by the beams of the three torches.

'And the King's Sword!' Emily shivered in awe as she took hold of the bejewelled pommel and pulled the sword from its scabbard. The blade glinted in the light. 'Wow! They're beautiful!'

Jack whistled. 'Yeah. The Pigster was right about one thing – this stuff does look even better in real life than on the poster.'

Scott's brain was buzzing on fast-forward. 'The thief must have hidden these here.'

Emily nodded sadly. 'Vicky White, supposedly. I still can't believe she did it.'

'I know,' Scott sighed. 'There's something odd about it. And I can't help wondering why she didn't come up with a better alibi . . . '

'But they found those security codes on her laptop,' Emily said. 'That definitely points the finger straight at Vicky . . .'

Suddenly Jack threw up his hands so suddenly he almost dropped the helmet. He'd figured it all out! '*Point the finger!* That's it! Aunt Kate was right. It *was* a set-up job. Someone's trying to make it look like Vicky did it.'

'But who would have framed her like that?' Emily asked.

'The Pigster, of course!' Jack cried. 'He copied the codes onto Vicky's laptop so the police would think she'd hacked into his computer. But he nicked the treasure himself! Then he brought it down the secret passage from the castle and hid it here.'

Emily grinned. 'You're right! That's what he was doing here when we saw him yesterday morning. No wonder he didn't look too pleased to see us! I wondered where he'd moored his boat, but he *didn't have one*. The secret passage meant he could get here in just a few minutes. It would've taken him at least half an hour by boat.'

'Oh, yes! Bow down in worship! We've cracked it!' Jack chanted, high-fiving with Emily, at least as far as it was possible to high-five while holding a torch and a Ceremonial Helmet.

'Er, sorry to break up the party,' Scott said, 'but you've forgotten something. Mrs Loveday could hear Mr Piggott in his office on both mornings. He *couldn't* have been down here.'

Jack stopped his victory dance and glared at him. Trust Scott Know-It-All Carter to pick holes in his theory. Why did Scott think he was the only one who had any brains around here, anyway? He desperately tried to think of a way to prove his brother wrong. Then it came to him. 'Mrs Loveday is *lying*. You can tell she's totally in love with The Pigster. I bet she's covering up for him.'

Emily giggled. 'Do you think they're, you know, having an affair?'

'Eugh! Pass the barf-bag,' Jack laughed.

'Well, I suppose they *could* be working together . . .' Scott admitted grudgingly.

Scott's voice trailed off as a volley of barking echoed round the cave.

'Drift's found something!' Emily cried.

The three friends directed their torch beams towards the sound. The little dog had ventured deeper into the cave. He had his nose to the ground and was scrabbling with his front paws. At first Emily couldn't see what it was, but she'd worked with Drift long enough to know that he didn't make a fuss over nothing. She knelt for a closer look. It was something small and shiny . . . Could it be more treasure?

She picked the tiny object up and held it out on her palm.

It was a crumpled ball of thin silver foil.

Jack grabbed it, smoothed it out and held it up to his torch. 'It's a chewing gum wrapper.' He examined it again. Printed across the foil like a watermark, he could just make out the logo: MegaMint.

Jack stared in disbelief. He'd been so sure that Piggott and Loveday were the thieves. He *wanted* it to be them, but he should have *known* the Pigster was too boring to do anything as daredevil as robbing a safe and making his getaway through a secret passage!

Scott was staring at the MegaMint wrapper too, slowly shaking his head. Jack could tell his brother was thinking the same thing.

They both knew who chewed this brand of gum.

It was hard to believe; he'd seemed like such a great guy. But the temptation of the Saxon treasure must have been too much.

It seemed Pete Morley hadn't given up his life of crime after all.

Seventeen

Inside the Cliff

Meanwhile, Emily was watching Drift. He was definitely on to something again. He paused at the base of a stack of rocks close to the site of the chewing gum find, held up one paw and sniffed the air. Then he scampered up the rocks, his ears telling Emily to follow him. She clambered up after him and shone her torch where Drift was looking. There it was! A hole in the wall the size of a small door, and beyond that a tunnel stretching back, deep into the cliff.

It was the most exciting moment of Emily's entire life!

'Drift's found the secret passage!' she shrieked.

Within seconds the boys were at her side.

'Way to go, Drifty!' Jack laughed. 'So, what are we waiting for?' With that, he launched himself head-first into the hole.

Scott grabbed him by the waistband of his shorts and yanked him back.

'What?' Jack protested. 'You scared or something?'

'Let's just think about this a minute.' The part of Scott's brain that dealt with common sense was doing battle with the part that desperately wanted to get into that secret passage and see where it went. *What if the roof collapses? Didn't Aunt Kate say the cliffs are crumbling dangerously?* But that was on the outside, not the inside. *What if there's no oxygen?* But Pete Morley must have made it through. *And then there's the rising tide . . .*

'How long have we got, Em?' Scott asked.

Emily shone her torch on her watch. 'About half an hour. We could check it out quickly. Make sure it's not a dead end. Then come back tomorrow for a more in-depth investigation.'

'See. *Emily's* not chicken,' Jack said.

Scott sighed. 'I'm not chicken. I just want to make it to my fourteenth birthday *alive*! OK, let's go in and have a look. But we'll be out of here in half an hour and I go first to make sure it's safe. Deal?'

Emily grinned. 'Deal.'

Jack stepped aside and bowed. 'After you!'

'OK, here goes.' Scott took a deep breath and entered the tunnel. It sloped steeply upwards. At first he had to crawl on all fours, trying to hold his torch at the same time. But then it opened out and he was able to walk – although hunched over – for a while. Jack, Emily and Drift were right behind him.

Scott focused on each step, holding back the blanket of panic that was threatening to suffocate him. The sound of his breathing was almost deafening. The air in the tunnel was whistling, resonating through his entire body. Suddenly, the hand he was holding out to feel the way ahead, struck something solid. He stopped and Jack and Emily both bumped into him.

'What's up?' Jack asked.

'Seems to be some kind of blockage,' Scott told him.

They all shone their torches ahead and saw an immense old wooden door, studded with nails and rivets and hanging on ancient iron hinges. Scott tried the huge iron handle. 'It's locked.'

Jack pushed past. 'Let me try. It's just like the door in the storeroom.' He wrenched the handle but it didn't budge. 'Stupid door!' He gave it a good kick. To his surprise, his trainer didn't meet the solid oak plank he had been expecting, but something soft and mushy like wet cardboard. 'Ughh! The wood's all rotten at the bottom.'

Drift started to scratch at the door with his paws. 'Good thinking, Drift,' Emily said. 'Maybe we can make a hole.' She knelt beside him and started to pry pieces of the plank away. Scott and Jack joined her.

'That's as much as we're going to get,' Scott panted after a few minutes' work. 'It's only that one small patch that's rotten. The rest of the wood is rock-solid!'

'Look, Drift's got through,' Jack pointed out. 'He thinks it's a dog-flap. Hey, Drifty, have a look and see if there's a key on that side, can you?'

Emily laughed. 'He's smart, but not that smart!'

'It's so unfair,' Jack groaned. 'Who put a door here, anyway?'

'Hang on, I think I can squeeze through.' Emily forced her shoulders through the splintered wood. She twisted, and pushed with her feet and, all at once, popped out into the other side of the tunnel. Drift yelped as she landed on top of him.

'Em, what can you see?' Scott yelled.

Emily shone her torch at the door. There was no key in the lock but it was bolted with two huge iron bolts. She reached up, grabbed the top one and pulled. There was a creak and she pulled harder. Suddenly the bolt shot back with a *clang*. Excitement pounded in her chest. *That bolt must have been oiled!* she thought. Which meant someone had been down here not long ago. She seized the second bolt. It opened just as easily. She put her shoulder to the door and pushed.

She was greeted by Jack, shining his torch under his chin and screwing his face up into a hideous grin. 'Trick or treaaaa . . . .' he began, but suddenly his voice tailed off. 'Wow! Amazing!'

The other two knew exactly what he meant. As soon as the door had swung open, the whistling vibrations in the air had ceased. Now all they could hear was water dripping softly from the walls of the tunnel.

'I was right!' Scott said. 'It's like an organ pipe. 'The whistling stops when this door is open.'

But Jack was already on his way. 'Never mind all that. Let's follow the rest of this passage and see where it comes out.'

Scott shone the torch on his watch. 'OK, just a few more minutes.'

They continued to make their way up the tunnel, which became steeper and darker and narrower. They were back on their hands and knees. Scott tried not to think about the tonnes of rock pressing down on top of them.

'Are we nearly there yet?' Jack joked.

We'd better be, Scott thought, *I can't go much further.* 'I think we'll have to turn round.' he whispered at last.

'No, look, it's opening out again,' Emily shouted, directing her torch over Scott's shoulder. 'I think this is the end of the passage.'

Scott looked up. Emily was right. The tunnel had led into a small chamber. 'Thank God,' he mumbled, staggering against the wall with relief.

'Aggh, my knees are shredded,' Jack groaned. 'Remind me to wear long trousers next time we do this.'

'Next time?' Scott spluttered. 'You think I'm *ever* doing this again?'

This is wild! Jack thought, as he scanned the walls for the entrance – and then the roof, which seemed to be made of huge flagstones. *I bet the secret passage comes out somewhere in the middle of the castle ruins. Now, where's the door?* Then he saw it. OK, it wasn't exactly a door, but still. Two grooves, just big enough for finger-holds, had been chiselled into one of the flagstones, and, *yes*, there were fresh scrape marks, white against the dark grey stone, along its length.

The stone must slide back!

A New Surprise

'Help me open it!' Jack shouted.

Scott and Emily rushed to his side and together they tried to push the solid stone to one side.

Suddenly Emily noticed that Drift had run to the back of the chamber and was sniffing the air at the mouth of the tunnel. His ears were tucked so tight against his head they were almost invisible. 'What's the matter, Drift?' she asked.

The little dog looked up at her with big dark eyes. Then he threw his head back and howled.

'It's not a full moon, you know, Drift,' Scott said.

Drift's howling got louder and louder. Then he started barking too, and running back and forth between Emily and the tunnel mouth.

'He wants to go back down,' Emily said. 'I'd better take him. Someone up top might hear all this howling.'

'We could all go back down and come back tomorrow?' Scott suggested.

'What?' Jack snorted. 'And leave without finding out where the secret passage comes out? You must be joking!'

Emily was longing to see what was on the other side of that stone slab too. She glanced at Drift. He was shaking from his nose to the tip of his tail. She looked at the slab again. Maybe Drift would be OK for a few more minutes. Now he was pawing at her legs. She'd never seen him so scared. She made up her mind. Drift was her top priority. 'Look. I'll go back down with Drift. You guys see if you can get that thing open. But don't stay long. Five minutes and then come back down before the water starts coming into the cave.'

'Are you sure you'll be OK in the passage on your own?' Scott asked.

'Of course. It'll be a doddle going down. We can slide on our bums most of the way. Anyway, I won't be on my own. I'll have Drift.'

'OK, we'll be five minutes behind you,' Scott said. Then he thought of something. 'And, Em?'

'What?'

'If the water starts coming in, you and Drift get out of there! Don't wait for us.'

—

Jack and Scott pushed and pushed until their arms were trembling.

At last the flagstone shifted a fraction. They heaved again and it slid further, grating over the neighbouring slab. But there was still something blocking out the light. Jack reached up and felt a bristly woven texture.

'It's a rug,' he whispered. 'We must be inside a room somewhere. Let me climb on your back. I'll roll it back.'

Scott looked horrified. 'A room? What if there's someone up there?'

'Hel-lo,' Jack laughed. 'If there's anyone home they'd have noticed us by now. Their rug will have been bouncing up and down like a flying carpet!'

'OK, just a quick peek and then we're out of here.'

At last Jack managed to push the rug to the side and light flooded in, dazzling him after so long in the darkness of the caves. He hoisted himself up and poked his head through the hole. He was in the corner of a room. As his eyes adjusted to the light he realized that the room was familiar: maps on the wall, shelves of dusty old books, a desk with a computer . . . He'd never forget this place. 'It's Mr Piggott's office!'

Cautiously, Scott poked his head out of the hole. He raked his hair out of his eyes and took a deep breath. They really *were* in Mr Piggott's office. He'd half-suspected Jack of making it up to wind him up. Now he thought about it, the museum offices were built into the old castle kitchens – the perfect place to have an escape tunnel in the olden days. 'But what I don't understand,' he said, 'is how Pete Morley found the secret passage hidden away in Mr Piggott's office? Perhaps he and Piggott are partners in crime? But we can work it out later. Right now we need to get back to Emily and out of that cave . . . Jack?' Scott looked around. He couldn't believe it. His stupid little brother had only climbed out of the hole and was wandering around the office.

'Jack!' Scott hissed, 'What are you *doing*?'

'Just having a quick reccy.'

'Get back here! Piggott might come back any second. Or Pete Morley. And the tide's coming in, remember?'

Sometimes, Jack thought, *it's hard to believe that Scott is older than me. He can be such a baby.* He carried on poking around amongst the papers on the desk. He wasn't sure what he was looking for. Just *something* to prove that Mr Piggott was the thief! He didn't want it to be Pete Morley. There was a copy of today's newspaper with Victoria White's face looking up from the front page. Jack picked it up and a pack of chewing gum fell out from the folds.

MegaMint chewing gum!

Suddenly Jack remembered Pete Morley's words as he offered his chewing gum around. *They're giving them away as freebies at the newsagent!* Of course! That meant everyone in Castle Key was chomping their way through MegaMint these days. Maybe even crusty old museum curators . . .

Jack looked in the wastepaper bin under the desk.

Three MegaMint chewing gum wrappers. Three balls of silver foil.

'Gotcha!' he shouted.

Jack held up the chewing gum to show Scott. 'I was right! It *was* The Pigster who stole the treasure. *He* dropped the silver foil in the cave.'

'Yes, alright! Now *come on!*' Scott lunged at Jack's ankle in a desperate rugby tackle, trying to drag him back through the hole.

'I'd like to speak to your Publicity Department please!'

Mr Piggott's voice blared out in the silent room. Jack jumped so high he could've broken an Olympic record. Apart from Scott sticking up through the hole like a startled meerkat, the office was empty!

'It's about the Carrickstowe Hoard Exhibition . . . '
Was Mr Piggott *hiding* somewhere? Was it a *ghost*? Terror turned Jack's stomach to ice and froze him to the spot.

'It's a recording on the computer,' Scott hissed, pointing at the speakers on the desk. 'You must have knocked the keyboard and set it off by mistake. Now *come on*, let's get out of here before he really does come back.'

Which was the precise second that Jack heard a key turn in the office door.

Eighteen

Distress Signal

E mily waited by the entrance to the secret passage. She checked her watch. She waited some more. She gave Drift a cuddle. He was still trembling and on edge, pacing around with his ears back. It was cold sitting in the cave on the stack of rocks. And dark. She wished she had her notebook to write up the new developments in the investigation. She couldn't wait to see D. I. Hassan's face when he found out that Emily had solved Operation Treasure – with a bit of help from Scott and Jack, of course. She checked her watch again. *Ten minutes.* Had the boys been able to shift that flagstone? It was *torture* not being up there with them, but Drift had howled so much she knew she'd done the right thing by coming back.

They'd been gone over fifteen minutes now. Emily crawled into the tunnel and shouted their names. There was no reply, except for the echo of her own voice and Drift howling again. 'It's OK,' she said, stroking his ears, 'I'm here.'

She sat down to wait again, but it was no good. She had to *do* something. 'Come on, Drift. We'll go and check on *Gemini*.' Emily had tied the mooring rope round the highest rock she could find, but there was still a chance that a rogue wave at high tide could wash the rope off the rock and set the boat adrift. And without it they would be stranded. Then she had an idea. She would take the treasure and stow it safely in the waterproof bag on the boat, ready for when the boys returned. She scooped up the heavy bundle and slid down the rock-pile.

Emily gasped as she landed in the freezing water. It was past her knees already. Not that she was worried about drowning or anything; she'd checked the tide-marks ringing the cave walls on their way in, of course. The water wouldn't get past shoulder-height. The only problem was the mouth of the outer cave. The roof dipped down sharply at the entrance so that at high tide it was totally submerged for a short time. You either had to swim out under water, or wait it out in the cave until the tide receded again.

But she couldn't help noticing the water was rising much faster than she'd expected. There was still half an hour until high tide. *Must be a spring tide,* she told herself. Old Bob had explained to her how the tides varied with the phases of the moon. They were always highest after a new or full moon.

Emily hoisted the sack of Saxon treasure onto her head and balanced it with one hand. In her other hand she held the torch. With Drift splashing along next to her, she waded across the cavern towards the narrow fissure in the wall that led to the outer cave. It was a tight squeeze with the bundle of treasure, but she made it through.

As soon as she came out into the outer cave, Emily knew something was wrong. Waves were rolling in fast and crashing against the walls. There was only a narrow band of daylight still remaining between the water and the roof at the entrance of the cave. Drift whimpered as a wave broke over him. Dropping her torch, Emily grabbed his collar and held on. She steadied herself against the wall. The water was washing past her waist now.

White light crackled across the cave-mouth like a camera flash.

Suddenly Emily knew what was happening. *Of course!* She should have seen it coming: the thunderbugs, the heat, the humid air . . . No wonder the waves were so massive: out in the bay a storm was raging!

She looked at Drift, swimming in the water next to her. Now she knew why he'd been so anxious to get out of the tunnel. He'd sensed the storm coming. It must have been the change in the air pressure or something. 'Oh, Drift, I'm sorry we didn't listen to you!'

She had to act fast. But what should she do? Get out while there was still a chance and save *Gemini* from being washed away by the storm? Or stay put in the cave and wait for the boys? Emily remembered Scott's words. *If the water starts coming in, don't wait for us.* But she couldn't just abandon her friends! And what if they were injured or in danger? Why else would they have been so long? She needed to get help, but she'd left her phone in the waterproof bag on *Gemini* – and she knew she wouldn't get a signal so close to the cliff, anyway. *There must be some way I can raise the alarm* . . . Then she remembered. *There are emergency flares in the boat!*

Emily's decision was made. 'Come on, Drift. Let's get out of here.'

Emily took a step forward, trying to hold the bundle of treasure up out of the water. But she lost her balance

146

and fell. Gasping for air, she surfaced, still clutching her cargo. But the sacking material was sodden and heavy. The artefacts had come unwrapped and kept falling out of the bundle.

Time was running out! Emily pulled off the remnants of the sack, took out the Ceremonial Helmet and placed it over her head. Inside it smelled of earth and metal and blood. It took a moment to line up the eye-slits, but as soon as she could see, she took the Chieftain's Shield in one hand and the King's Sword in the other and holding them both up out of the water, she forded the chest-high waves like a warrior princess.

With Drift swimming valiantly alongside, Emily headed for the light at the cave-mouth. There was barely enough room for their heads to stay above water as they made it through to the open sea. Now where was *Gemini*? But before she could get her bearings a titanic wave swept her off her feet. Another crashed over her head. Now the helmet was filling with water. Emily choked and spluttered as the water rushed up her nose. Fighting for breath, she let go of the shield and sword and tugged at the helmet. Somehow she managed to pull it free. Half-blind with salt water and bright light, she looked around for Drift. There he was, swimming towards her, his legs paddling frantically, a look of pure terror in his eyes.

Suddenly Emily saw her boat. *Gemini* was being tossed around by the waves, like a mouse between a cat's paws, but at least it was still attached to the mooring rope. In one move, Emily grasped hold of the bow and threw the helmet over the side. Then she turned back and grabbed Drift by the scruff of his neck. With a surge of super-human strength, she lifted him out of the surf and propelled him towards the boat, where, with a mad scrabble of paws and a shove from below, he was able to make it over the side to safety. Emily was just starting to haul herself up after him when she remembered the shield and the sword.

The shield was floating on a wave and she reached out and grabbed it. She looked around in a panic but there was no sign of the sword anywhere. *I've lost the King's Sword!* she thought miserably.

Emily felt her body growing heavier and heavier as the last shreds of energy ebbed away. The sword had sunk beneath the waves. And now she was being pulled down too . . . down . . . under . . . the sea. She couldn't fight it . . . But then she heard something. It was the sound of barking. *Drift needs me! Scott and Jack need me!* Somehow, Emily dragged herself up and over the side to land flat on her face in the water sloshing at the bottom of the boat.

Drift licked her ear.

Exhausted and shaking with cold, Emily felt under the seat for the emergency supplies.

She pulled out the spare ropes, a life-ring and a flare. If ever there was time for a distress signal, this was it!

Twenty

A Narrow Escape

J ack didn't hang around to say hello to Mr Piggott.

He rocketed into the secret passage, reached up and started tugging on the stone slab.

'Don't bother trying to close it,' Scott said urgently, pulling him down. 'We can't put the rug back over so Piggott's going to be on to us anyway!'

Jack launched himself into the tunnel and began to hurtle down the steep incline as fast as he could. It was like one of those bobsleigh races he'd seen on the Winter Olympics – except the track was *inside* the mountain, in the dark, and he'd forgotten to bring a sleigh!

Jack's thoughts were racing too. There could no longer be any doubt. The Pigster – not Pete Morley – had stolen the Saxon treasure and hidden it in the cave. He'd obviously had it all planned out. He'd even recorded those phone conversations to trick Mrs Loveday into thinking he was in his office when he was *actually* scooting off down the secret passage. And then he'd framed Victoria White for the crime by copying the security codes onto her laptop. Jack had to admit it, the guy was *clever* – and far less boring than he'd given him credit for.

'What was that?' Scott shouted. Jack had heard it too. A noise in the tunnel behind them. Mr Piggott had climbed into the secret passage.

'Hurry up!' Scott yelled.

'What d'you think I'm doing? Stopping off for an ice cream or something?' Jack panted. Of course he was hurrying. Something told him The Pigster wasn't going to be at all happy that they'd uncovered his little secret! *At least we've got a head start,* Jack thought. *And Mr Piggott is old. Unless he's some kind of geriatric Superman, he'll have to take it a bit more slowly. By the time he gets down to the caves we'll be rowing off in the boat with Emily, on our way to call the police . . .*

At last the boys tumbled out of the tunnel. 'Emily!'

Scott yelled. 'Drift!' There was no reply.

'They must be waiting for us in *Gemini*!' Jack said, scrambling down the rocks. 'Come on.'

Scott started to follow. Then he heard a splash and a scream. He shone his torch down to see Jack with swirling water halfway up his *Simpsons* t-shirt.

'Water's coming in!' Jack's voice was shrill with fear. 'We're going to drown!'

Scott's heart was beating faster than in a penalty shoot-out. He had no idea how fast the water was rising or how high it would get. But he forced himself to sound calm. 'Don't panic. We've just got to wade through it and out to the boat.'

Jack gulped and nodded.

Together they made their way across the cavern, holding their torches up to light the way. Scott noticed the beams were dwindling. The batteries wouldn't last much longer. He decided this wasn't the time to mention it to Jack. And as soon as they'd squeezed through the gap in the wall, there'd be light coming in from outside anyway.

But Scott was wrong! When they emerged into the outer cave it was dark. Even worse, the water was deeper here, with waves surging in and breaking against the walls. Scott's feet were only just touching the ground. Jack was already out of his depth, clinging round Scott's neck like velcro. Scott directed his feeble torch beam to where the cave-mouth *should* be. They were trapped!

The tide had risen past the top of the entrance.

'Scott?' Jack whimpered. 'Let's go back.'

Scott nodded. Compared to drowning, crawling back up that horrible tunnel and being caught by Mr Piggott didn't sound so bad. But as he turned back, his torch emitted one last flicker of light and went out. Seconds later, Jack's torch failed too.

'Scott! What are we going to do?' Jack tightened his grip.

'It's OK. It's OK,' Scott mumbled, prising Jack's fingers away from his windpipe. But it wasn't OK. A metallic taste of fear filled his mouth. *It's pitch dark. How are we going to find our way back to the secret passage?* He couldn't even see the gap through to the inner cave. Scott closed his eyes. *How did I let this happen?*

He opened his eyes. Then he noticed something. It was dark, but it *wasn't* pitch dark. Light was coming through the water near the cave-mouth. Yes, it was a faint, greyish light, but it *was* light. And that meant that the water covering the cave-mouth couldn't be that deep! They could swim through underwater and pop out the other side – but they'd have to be quick. The water was getting deeper by the minute. The hard part was going to be persuading Jack. Jack was perfectly capable of swimming – even if he did have all the style of a demented poodle – but, right now, fear had turned him into a gelatinous blob.

'Jack!' Scott spoke slowly and firmly as if talking to a naughty toddler. 'I'm going to tell you what to do. We're going to be fine. But you have to do *exactly* what I say, OK?'

Clinging on to Scott, Jack flailed his way through the churning water. He had no idea how Scott was going to get them out of here, but he'd given up trying to think. They'd reached the other side of the cave now. Scott was yelling something at him again. He tried to focus through the fog of fear.

'We're going to swim out underwater. I'll go first and check how far it is. I'll come back for you in a minute. Hang on tight to the wall.'

Swim underwater? Jack shook his head. 'I can't!' But Scott had already gone.

Jack waited. How long had it been? If he stayed here the water might rise up to the roof of the cave. Something must have happened to Scott. He had to go and see. He had to swim under the water. Under the rock. Fear was inflating inside Jack's chest like a balloon. *Just pretend you're on that rope swing under the willow tree again,* he told himself. *Now you're jumping into the river . . .*

Jack sucked in a great lungful of air and plunged head-first beneath the waves. *Kick hard . . . Can't breathe . . . Keep swimming . . . Got to get out . . .*

Through the churning depths, Jack saw a tunnel and a flash of white light . . . *This must be the end . . .* But then something was seizing him in a whooshing whirlpool of bubbles and water and coughing and thrashing . . . *It's a shark . . . No, that's a hand. Sharks don't have hands* . . . 'Scott?'

'I was on my way back for you, you dumbo!' Scott was shouting in his ear as they surfaced. 'And stop strangling me!'

'I was going towards the white light . . . '

'Yeah, it's called lightning,' Scott spluttered as a wave the size of a skateboard ramp crashed over them.

Then there was another light. Orange, this time, shooting up into the sky.

'Scott! Jack!' Emily's voice carried across the waves. 'Catch . . . '

Jack grabbed hold of the life-ring. Moments later, he was lying, curled up with a very bedraggled Drift, in the bottom of the boat. *Gemini* was rocking around like a bucking bronco but Jack didn't care. He was out of the water! He could hear Scott and Emily talking. Snippets of their conversation wafted down to him through the howling wind and lashing rain . . . *Distress flare . . . Storm . . . Mr Piggott's office . . . Sword . . .*

Then he heard what sounded like Emily crying. This wasn't right! Emily didn't *cry*! 'I dropped the sword!' she sobbed. 'In the water . . . it's lost . . . '

Jack sat bolt upright. 'Lost the sword?' he asked.

Emily nodded. Her dark curls were plastered across her face like seaweed. Scott put his arm round her. 'It's OK. It wasn't your fault.'

Jack stared in amazement. It wasn't the fact that Scott had his arm round a girl – after all, Emily didn't really *count* as a girl. His eyes had locked onto something behind Scott's left shoulder; poking out from a crevice in the cliff-face, not far from the rock where the mooring rope was tied, was a gleam of gold!

'Jack! What are you doing?'

Before Scott or Emily could stop him Jack was sliding over the bow of the boat and pulling himself along the mooring rope through the foaming waves. He clambered up onto the rock and grabbed hold of a spur jutting out further up on the outcrop. *Dry land!* This was more like it! He groped for a handhold and pulled himself up, then wedged his toe into a tiny crack in the cliff-face. A couple more moves and he was able to reach out and snag the hilt of the sword. He gave it a tug and it slid out from the rock. *Wow! This must be how King Arthur felt when he pulled the sword out of the stone*, Jack thought. He couldn't resist holding it up and shouting, 'Excalibur!'

Climbing down one-handed was harder, but he made it. 'Is this the item you were looking for, Madam?' he asked, holding up the sword as Emily and Scott man-handled him back over the side of the boat.

Emily was still crying, but now she was laughing and hugging him at the same time. 'The waves must have washed it up there.'

'You *idiot!*' Scott snapped. 'You could've been killed

if you'd fallen off those rocks!'

Jack grinned. Scott was yelling at him for taking stupid risks. Things were back to normal. With luck, Jack's Extreme Wimpiness Attack in the cave need never be spoken of again!

'Look, there's a boat coming,' Emily shouted. 'They must have seen the flare.' She wobbled her way to the stern and peered out across the storm-curdled bay. 'It's Old Bob's fishing boat!'

Twenty one

Return to Castle Key

Scott, Jack and Emily were soon huddled in the cabin of the fishing boat heading back to Castle Key harbour. Wrapped in blankets and drinking strong tea from Old Bob's flask, they were warm and sleepy. Drift was snuggled up next to Emily and *Gemini* was being towed along behind. The old fisherman had raised one bushy eyebrow beneath his woolly hat when he'd helped them aboard and they'd handed him the Chieftain's Shield, the Ceremonial Helmet and the King's Sword to stow below deck.

'Been out on a treasure hunt?' he asked.

'Something like that!' Scott replied.

Old Bob nodded slowly. 'I was heading ashore to get out of the storm when I noticed the whistling had ceased – just like young Emily said the other day. I was looking over at the caves when I saw the flare go up. Thought I'd better come and see who'd got themselves into a spot of bother.'

'Cheers!' Jack said. 'Thanks for rescuing us.'

'Bob, can you radio for the police?' Emily asked. 'There's something we need to report.'

'Quicker to use this.' Old Bob pulled a new-model iPhone out of his pocket. 'Should get a signal any second now. Storm's passing over already. Ah, there we go.'

'It'll be too late,' Jack said. 'The Pigster will be on his way back up the secret passage by now.'

Scott sighed. Jack was right. It would take the police twenty minutes to drive from Carrickstowe Station to the castle. Mr Piggott would be long gone. Somehow they had to stop him leaving the castle. Then he had an idea. 'Bob, do you know a man called Pete Morley?'

'Aye,' Old Bob chuckled. 'Stan Morley's lad. Bit of a tearaway in his time.'

'Can you get his number?'

'Should have it in my contacts list,' Bob muttered, his gnarled fingers scrolling down the numbers. 'Pete did a bit of work on my fence for me last year. Here it is. It's ringing.' He handed the phone to Scott.

'Pete! It's Scott Carter,' Scott rattled the words out as quickly as he could. 'Yeah, I helped you with those tiles yesterday. This is an emergency. Are you at the castle? Great. Can you stand guard outside Mr Piggott's office? Don't let him leave. The police are on their way.'

Scott hung up. 'He says he'll be happy to!'

—

Next morning, Emily was curled up with Drift on her favourite sofa in the family living room on the sixth floor of The Lighthouse, gazing through the window at the sea – now blue and calm again – and writing up her notes on Operation Treasure. She'd already given the police a statement, but she'd promised to have a full case report on Detective Inspector Hassan's desk by the end of the day. At first Emily had been afraid she'd be in trouble for getting the Saxon artefacts wet, but it seemed the British Museum were just pleased to have the treasure back at all. And, after all, the Carrickstowe Hoard had been buried under a cow field for over a thousand years; a quick dip in the sea wasn't going to hurt it.

There was a ring of the bell downstairs and Mum shouted for Scott and Jack to come on up.

'Hey, dudes! How's it going?' Dad looked up from

the table where he was doing the accounts. 'Heard about your little adventure yesterday.'

Emily grinned. The three of them had made a pact that they were going to give Emily's parents and Aunt Kate the PG version of the 'spot-of-bother' they'd got into at the caves yesterday. She hadn't *lied* to them, of course, but Parental Guidance said it was always best to leave out a few of the more hair-raising bits to avoid the risk of panic.

'It's cool how you guys stumbled on that Saxon treasure while you were exploring in the caves,' Dad said. 'Sounds like you got a bit damp when that storm blew up though!'

'Come on, Seth,' Mum said, 'let's leave these kids to themselves. We need to get to Carrickstowe market before all the best organic vegetables have been snapped up.'

'Have you got them?' Emily asked as soon as her parents were safely out of the way.

Scott nodded and handed over the newspapers. Geoff Piggott's arrest was on the front page – not only of *The Carrickstowe Times*, but of the national papers too. 'Oh, and we've got six free packs of MegaMint as well,' Scott said, tipping the chewing gum out of the carrier bag.

They read in silence for a few moments.

'Wow! The Pigster's confessed to *everything*!' Jack laughed. 'Wish I could have been a fly on the wall when

162

he came up the secret passage and found Pete Morley waiting for him in his office – followed by half the Cornish police force!'

Emily looked up from the article she was reading. 'The problem with this case,' she said seriously, 'was that we could never establish a motive for Mr Piggott. But he had one all along!'

It was all there in black and white. When the local metal detector enthusiast, Mervyn Heslop, discovered the Carrickstowe Hoard all those years ago, he'd used the research in Geoff Piggott's books and articles to work out where the burial site was likely to be located. According to Mr Piggott, they had a verbal agreement to split the proceeds of any finds. But when the Hoard was sold to the British Museum, Mervyn Heslop went back on his word and took off to a life of luxury in the Caribbean. Of course, the White family had also been entitled to a large cut of the money, since the treasure was found on their farmland – money that Geoff Piggot felt was rightfully *his*. Framing Victoria White for the crime was his way of exacting revenge.

'And, of course, being a museum curator, he'd know the value of the artefacts,' Scott said. 'He must have found a contact to sell them on to.'

'I bet Mrs Loveday is heartbroken,' Jack sighed. 'Her darling Mr Piggott is the Criminal Elephant after all!'

The bell rang again.

Victoria White ran up the stairs and scooped Emily

up in a hug. 'I saw in the papers how you found the treasure!'

'Oh, well, it was just lucky we happened to be exploring in the caves . . . ' Emily said.

Vicky smiled. 'And you just *happened* to stumble on the secret passage up to Geoff Piggott's office, as well, I suppose? It's OK. I know all about it. Pete Morley told me how Scott called to tell him to guard the office. I can't believe Piggott tried to blame the crime on me. He sent me on that bogus appointment in Carrickstowe and copied the security codes onto my laptop! Anyway, I'd have been in prison if it wasn't for you guys. But don't worry,' she added, grinning, 'I won't tell anyone if you want to keep a low profile. Now, what are you guys doing tomorrow?'

'Dunno,' Scott said. 'Thought we might have a quiet day. Do a bit of light *swimming*?' he shot a look at Jack.

'Or maybe a bit of rock-climbing,' Jack fired back. 'Pot-holing even?'

'Would you like to come over to Roshendra Farm for the day?' Vicky asked.

Jack hesitated. Farms were messy and smelly and always sounded like hard work, what with all that digging and planting and muck-spreading . . .

'It's just that we're branching out into making our own dairy ice cream, and we really need someone to come and test all the new flavours . . . '

'Now you're talking!' Jack laughed.

'See you tomorrow then,' Vicky called as she hurried off.

Emily got up from the sofa, sending the newspapers tumbling onto the floor. She stretched. 'Well, Drift and I have some Undercover Surveillance to do this afternoon.' She paused and grinned. 'Of course, you two could come along – if you're interested in assisting me on another investigation, that is.'

'Ooh, yes!' Jack said. 'What is it?' In his mind they were already hunting down violent bank-robbers and coldblooded blackmailers.

'It's an ongoing investigation,' Emily said. 'I had to put it on the back-burner while we focused on Operation Treasure. It's called Operation Spy Ring.'

Drift's ears stood to attention. *Operation* was one of his favourite words. It meant more exciting adventures.

'Smashing!' Jack laughed, rubbing his hands together.

Scott grinned. 'Smashing!' he echoed. *If it has anything to do with Emily Wild*, he thought, *it probably will be.*

Summer in Castle Key wasn't turning out to be so bad after all!

Don't miss the next exciting mystery
in the *Adventure Island* series

THE MYSTERY OF THE
MIDNIGHT GHOST

Available now!

Read on for a special preview of the first chapter.

One

An Exciting Arrival

'**Y**ou'll *never* guess who's just checked in at The Lighthouse!' Emily shouted into her mobile phone, before Scott even had a chance to say hello.

'Nelson Mandela?' Scott suggested. 'David Beckham? No, don't tell me, the Queen . . .'

Emily laughed. The boys would never guess in a million years! She jumped up and grabbed her binoculars from the box marked *Operations Kit* under her bed. There were three windows in the curved walls of her bedroom, all small and round like a ship's portholes. One looked out to a sky full of seagulls and a sparkling blue sea stretching to the horizon. The next framed Key Bay with its towering cliffs, topped by the jagged outline of the castle ruins. But it was the third window she ran to now, with its view of Castle Key far below, tiny as a model village. Tucked behind the church she could make out Stone Cottage, where her new friends Scott and Jack Carter were spending the summer with their Aunt Kate. Having your bedroom on the top floor of a lighthouse was a definite plus for all-round surveillance!

'Lady Gaga? Johnny Depp?' It was Jack's voice now. Emily pictured him wrestling the phone out of his older brother's hand. 'Winnie the Pooh?'

Winnie the Pooh? If Jack was moving on to *fictional* characters, they could be here for weeks! Emily couldn't bear it any longer – it was like giving someone an amazing Christmas present and then having to watch while they opened it in slow motion, trying not to tear the paper. 'It's an ex-SAS commando,' she blurted.

'Yeah, right!' Scott had grabbed his phone back from Jack. 'And I suppose James Bond will be popping in later for your mum's buffet lunch!'

Emily was used to Scott teasing her. She did a backwards dive onto her bed. 'His name's Max Fordham. He was in the Gulf War and he's done loads of secret operations.' Then she screamed as a blur of black and tan and white fur launched itself onto her stomach. 'Drift! It's not a game,' she giggled. A rescue dog of unknown origin, Drift was the perfect combination of the best bits of every breed – the brains of a collie, the bounce of a spaniel, the bravado of a Jack Russell – and he was Emily's constant companion.

In the sunny kitchen at Stone Cottage, Scott shook his head at his mobile and grinned at his brother. 'According to Em, a member of the SAS has just checked in at The Lighthouse.'

'SAS? As in Special Air Service?' Jack spluttered through a mouthful of bacon. It was still early and they were working their way through one of Aunt Kate's immense cooked breakfasts. 'As in *Who Dares Wins* and all that? Cool!'

Scott shrugged. Emily was always imagining secret agents, kidnappers and gangsters around every corner! If Winnie the Pooh *did* turn up at her parents' Bed and Breakfast at The Lighthouse, Emily would suspect him of masterminding an international honey-smuggling ring. Her SAS commando was probably just a guy with muscles in camo-pattern trousers.

'How do you *know* he's SAS?' Scott asked, switching his phone to speaker so that Jack could hear. 'Did he storm in through the window brandishing a machine gun?'

'When he was signing the register I noticed he had

this little tattoo on his arm,' Emily explained patiently. 'A dagger with wings on it. That's the SAS insignia.'

Scott had to admit he was impressed. Emily noticed things. She noticed things most people wouldn't notice even if they were waving a red flag and doing a Mexican Wave.

'So I asked him,' Emily went on, 'and he told me all about it. He's really nice. Drift likes him too!' As far as Emily was concerned Drift was never wrong about such things.

'But what's he doing in Castle Key?' Scott asked. 'They haven't discovered a terrorist cell operating out of Dotty's Tea Rooms have they?'

'I told you, Max isn't in the SAS any more. He's a civilian now.' Emily shook her head. Sometimes talking to the boys could be like walking up a down escalator!

In the kitchen at Stone Cottage, Jack let a piece of bacon fall off his fork. 'So he's just here on *holiday*? Yawn!'

'Ah, but I haven't told you the Most Amazing Part of All yet!' Emily said in a mysterious tone. 'Meet me at the end of the harbour wall in ten minutes.'

Scott did a double take at his phone. Emily had rung off already. He raised his eyebrows in Jack's direction.

But Jack was already at the door. Bubbles of excitement were fizzing in his stomach. If Emily said something was *amazing*, it was *guaranteed to* be good! Then he ran back into the kitchen and snagged a piece of toast to eat on the way. 'What are we waiting for?' he asked, tugging Scott by the scruff of his t-shirt.

'Calm down!' Scott got up from his chair with all the speed of a sleep-walking snail. Scott liked to appear ice-cool and unruffled in all situations. It drove Jack crazy! Especially when he knew that beneath the laid-back pose, Scott was just as keen to find out Emily's news as he was.

The boys headed down Church Lane, along the high street, and through Fish Alley onto the seafront. The narrow streets of the old fishing village were familiar territory now, although Scott and Jack had only arrived in Castle Key a few weeks ago. They'd been packed off to stay with their Great-aunt Kate while Dad was spending the summer at an archaeological site in Africa digging up old pots. At first Jack had thought he'd die of boredom – a million miles from London and his friends – stuck in the middle of nowhere on an island he'd never even heard of off the coast of Cornwall.

But then the boys met Emily Wild, and the next thing they knew, they were swept up in Operation Treasure, tracking down a stolen Saxon sword, helmet and shield. OK, so getting trapped in a pitch black cave in a storm with the tide rising by the second was *not* an experience Jack wanted to repeat any time soon, but the rest of it had been awesome! Since then, things had been a little quiet. They'd been assisting Emily with her ongoing investigation, Operation Spy Ring. Unfortunately, despite the exciting name, it hadn't turned out to have quite the thrill-factor Jack had hoped for, mainly involving staking out the Post Office and watching people buying stamps. It was high time for a new adventure.

The boys hurried along the pebble beach where they were met by Drift, springing around their ankles like a hyperactive grasshopper. Emily was waiting for them, perched on the wall, hugging her knees to her chest, her jumble of long brown curls curtaining her face.

'What's the Most Amazing Part of All?' Jack panted.

Emily grinned at the boys' eager faces. They were already looking less London and more Castle Key; the sun had brought out freckles on Jack's nose and streaked Scott's floppy brown hair with surfer-dude highlights. 'You've heard of the Agent Diamond films, right?'

'*Heard* of them!' Jack laughed, sitting down next to Emily on the limpet-encrusted wall. 'They're only my all-time favourite movies! *The Diamond Mission* was the best. That's the one where Maya Diamond has to find Dr Zoltan's secret underwater lair . . .'

'No way!' Emily shoved Jack so he almost toppled backwards off the wall, '*The Diamond Code* was the classic. Where Maya has to go undercover as a double agent in Russia . . .'

Scott laughed and held up his hands. 'Cease fire! We *all* rate the Agent Diamond films, but what have they got to do with your SAS guy?'

174

Emily shaded her eyes and gazed out across the bay, pausing for maximum effect. 'They're going to film some scenes for the next movie on location here at the castle! Max Fordham is their stunt advisor.'

'*Agent Diamond?* Filming *here*?' Jack echoed. This was *officially* the single most exciting thing that had ever happened in the history of the universe.

'When?' Scott asked. He was trying to sound casual, but Jack could tell he was stoked too.

'They start filming in a couple of days.' Emily hopped down from the wall and started strolling casually away from the harbour. Drift trotted along behind, his velvety ears bobbing up and down in time with his paws.

'Where are you going?' Scott called.

Emily turned and spoke as she continued to walk backwards. 'Max said we could go up to the castle and watch him set up the stunts. That's if you're interested, of course . . .'

'*If* we're interested? Jack laughed. '*If*?' He sprang down from the wall and rocketed after Emily. Scott was not far behind.

Watching an SAS commando rigging up impossibly dangerous stunts for a high-octane action thriller – Jack had never been more interested in anything in his entire life!